Just Above Water

JUST ABOVE WATER

Edited by
Racquel Henry
Marquita Hockaday
and Kip Wilson

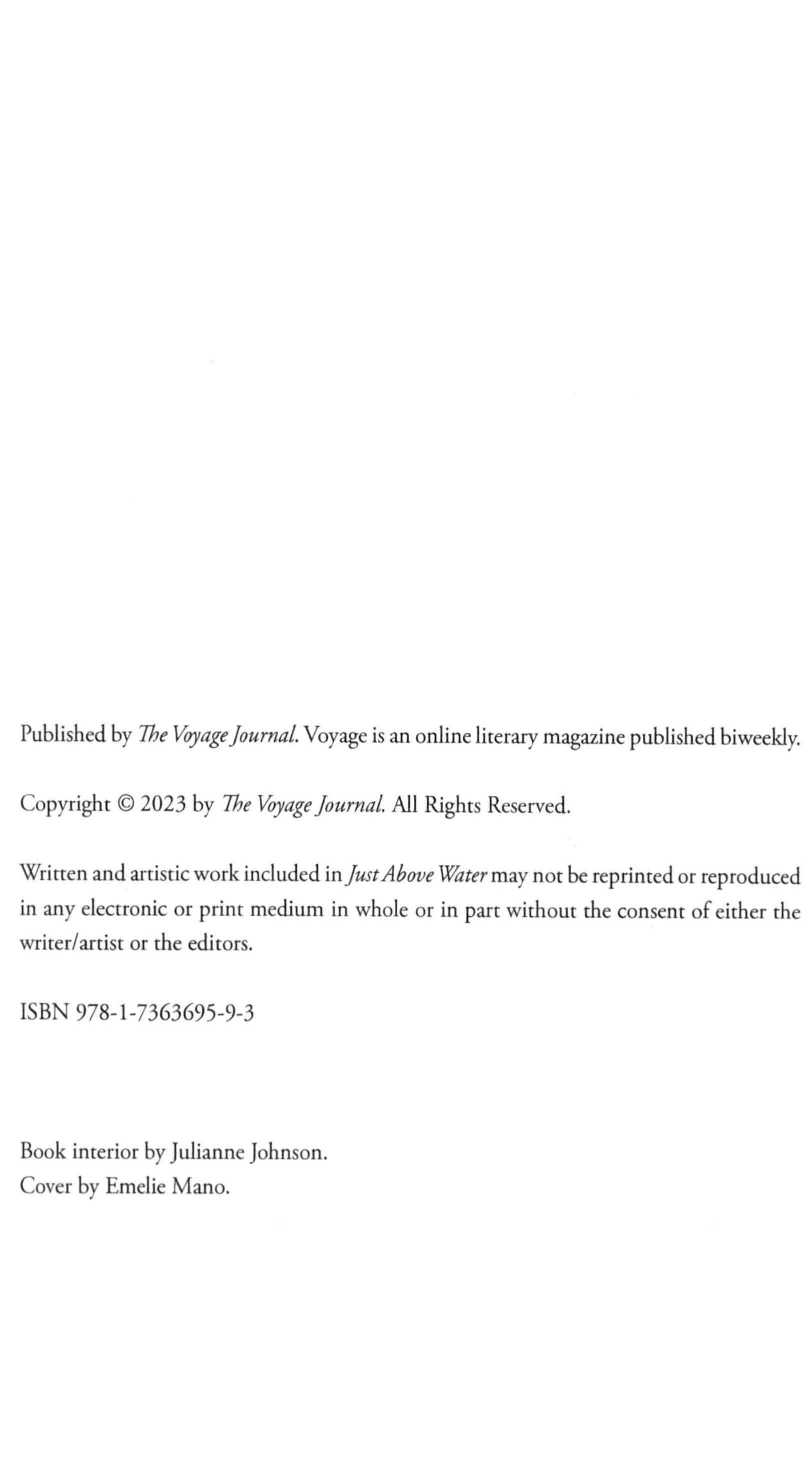

Published by *The Voyage Journal*. Voyage is an online literary magazine published biweekly.

ISBN 978-1-7363695-9-3

Book interior by Julianne Johnson.
Cover by Emelie Mano.

1. BOYZ N THE WOODS
Kim Johnson

13. ANIOMALLIA
Brynne Rebele-Henry

20. LAST DANCE (ABOVE WATER)
Madelin A. Medina

22. A BEAUTIFUL PARADOX
Kate Larkindale

32. ARTEMIS//APOLLO
Christina Polge

33. OUR CORRESPONDENCE
Maia Cataldo

60. LIKE THIS
Valerie Kemp

62. PETALS FALLING
Rieko Mendez

80. SAY MY NAME LIKE A PRAYER
CeCe Heard

82. THE NIGHT SEARCH
Andrea Lianne Grabowski

95. CONTRIBUTORS
99. EDITORS

BOYZ N THE WOODS

Kim Johnson

IT WAS BECAUSE OF DAD we were in the woods. He'd much rather know we were out in the wilderness than out on the streets—even if they weren't anything like when he was growing up.

"Watch this." I skipped a rock that sent ripples across the water. Jay stopped to give me a dap before making his own sad attempt, never having mastered the art of a good flick of the wrist and a whole lot of patience. Dad was the one who taught me, but back then Jay never had the patience. He was always complaining about the conditions. *It'd be better at a lake. The wind was picking up. I always somehow get the good rocks.* The river looked smooth and easy, like you could swim all the way north or float undisturbed in place. Underneath the thick and dark water, though, lay a current that could catch you by surprise on the wrong day.

"Why didn't Ricky zigzag?" Jay planted his feet closer to the edge of the river before launching a pebble into the abyss.

"What?" I scrunched up my face.

"Ricky Ricky." He gestured wildly with his hands, face stone cold serious.

I blew out a harsh breath because it was obvious who he was talking about, so I just kept throwing rocks.

"You know." Jay mimicked the motion of throwing a football, then moved his hands like he was running. "Ricky."

"Not this again." I squatted, searching for a flat rock. I smiled when I found a good one and rubbed the mud off before running my thumb over it to feel how smooth it was. "At some point you gotta let it go lil bro."

"Never." His jaw went tight at my betrayal to differentiate our ages.

He hated it when I called him lil bro. He's so used to us being known as the Black Irish twins he'd completely forget we weren't literal twins, we were just born ten months apart. Yeah, we're replicas of our dad, always together, our style indistinguishable, and even shared the same class when fourth and fifth grade was grouped together—but we weren't actual twins.

"You know you'll never find the answer you're looking for," I said. "Besides, Ricky's last moves can't really get to you like this, can they? I think you're just trying to get under my skin."

"No for real, Gary. It really bothers me." His expression dulled, but I didn't answer him, unsure what to say.

Today Jay'd been all about trying to make sense of the senseless. Gun violence. Death. Racism. Police brutality. And of course, if Ricky had a scholarship to USC as a running back, why'd he run a straight shot rather than a zigzag move during the drive by scene in *Boyz n the Hood.*

"I don't know, man. It was messed up, though." I finally gave in just to stop his moping. I didn't put extras on it though. Besides, we'd been at this for hours, solving the world's problems one issue at a time.

The first time we watched *Boyz n the Hood* was seven years ago in Dad's basement. And we'd been at this question ever since. Back then at ten years old, the basement was our pretend bachelor pad with us sneaking in the mini fridge for sodas, feet up on an old leather coach, and flicking through old DVDs. At first sight watching *Boyz n the Hood*, we thought the movie was about Robin Hood or a rap group. Even better, Rapping Robin Hood. The second it was on we were mesmerized until we realized Dad would whoop us if he caught us watching an R-rated movie.

"Well—" Jay started, eyeing the calm water.

"Here we go," I said under my breath.

Jay gave me an eyeroll and kept talking, "He had a division one scholarship."

"And?" I flicked another rock, feeling the cool breeze on my skin.

"Instinct would've had him flying in reversals and flipping over fences."

"He wasn't running a play," I said.

"But he ran a straight shot in the middle of the road." Jay clapped between each syllable for emphasis. "Like come on. If he would've shook 'em a little bit, he would've been sitting pretty headed off to college."

"It's a movie. Ricky wasn't supposed to go to college."

"But why though? Why couldn't he?"

I threw my head back letting another harsh breath come out. "Because Tre's supposed to. How many times do I gotta explain this. Ricky's death was necessary to symbolize the Black American dream coming up short."

"Why?"

"Because, well, racism." I shrugged my shoulders at the obvious.

"That makes no sense. Why him?"

"First off, if his brother Doughboy got shot it'd be too expected, end up a whole different type of movie. Second, with Ricky it was the injustice of it, it got us outraged. Got you thinking about it still. Third, if it was Tre, it'd be no movie."

"But Ricky got shot by gang members in a retaliation, not cops."

I bit my lip, thinking over if I really wanted to go into this with him. I looked over and he was stuck in place, rock in hand, waiting for me to answer. Behind him a black-tailed deer stepped gingerly from the backdrop of green flush trees only fifty yards away. When I was younger, I was cautious with my movements not to scare deer away, until I realized it was hard to get them to run because they're so used to people. But I was still mesmerized each time I saw them. I turned to Jay, ready to switch the conversation to the outdoors and play a game of spotthewildlife bingo. Eagle. Heron. Salmon. Duck. Beaver. But he was still looking at me to answer him. Some kids ran up on the deer excited, which caused it to scatter quickly in leaping bounds. I lowered my shoulders, forced to get back to Jay.

"You gotta go deeper. The movie covered cops, poverty, systemic issues that cycle through if you don't ever get a leg up. Remember what Tre's dad, Furious Styles, was saying in the movie? About how did crack get in the neighborhood in the first place since we don't own the planes or the access to get it out there. And who owns the liquor stores and why they're allowed on every corner only in our neighborhoods. And gentrification. Get the property value so low people gotta sell, then raise the rates right on up so they make money." I went through a list of things he already knew. Reminding him play by play what the whole movie already covered. What we'd already covered.

This fool still looked at me and said, "But why'd Ricky have to go out like that?"

"Why does it matter?"

"It matters." Jay threw a rock down and the water splashed my shoes.

I stepped back. "Hey, watch it."

"You're standing on rocks on a dirty bank, what do your shoes getting a little bit wet matter?"

"Don't mean I want to ruin 'em."

Jay picked up a handful of rocks, and it's like everything went slow motion because I just didn't believe he was about to do what I thought he was. His face turned cold, and he brought his arm back with a force so quick I could only watch it happen.

Split splat.

Mud and rocks didn't just hit the water, they hit my shoes too. The shock of his action wore off within seconds, and I lunged for him only grasping his shirt as he fought me off. Unable to get away from me, I put him in a headlock.

"What's wrong with you, man?" I held on tighter, waiting for him to call mercy.

But he kept on resisting. A few more seconds went by, and I realized he wasn't fighting me anymore—he was sobbing.

I let go.

Jay turned his back against me heaving over as he caught his breath in between guttural sounding cries. I slapped his back, let him know I was still here for him. I thought he was about to apologize until he jammed his shoulder into my chest, slamming the wind out of me. He heaved so hard I was knocked in midair before landing flat on my back. The water sunk deep into my toes, and my shorts pockets filled with water. I struggled to catch my breath while keeping my head above water, so I wouldn't get drenched. Jay's face was so filled with rage at first, I was ready to attack, but then he went back to crying. When I saw this, I couldn't even get mad at him. Because this wasn't Jay. None of it. Not the anger. Not the tears for no reason.

I swallowed hard, knowing this hadn't been about Ricky. It was all about Dad. Why'd *this* have to happen to Dad. My insides felt raw and vulnerable and that ache I'd been swallowing in the back of my throat threatened to release the sadness I'd buried to be strong for Jay.

Jay hadn't been ready to talk about Dad. Really, neither of us had. That's why we're here, ditching school today when we'd never ditched in our life. Dad would've never let us get away with that. But Dad wasn't here. So, I did the only thing I knew how to do. I dunked on this fool and brought Jay down so we'd be even. And when he was good and full on wet, I let him up.

Let silence take over between us.

Let the water-rushing sounds of the stream bring my heart rate down.

Let the fresh air fill my lungs, prepare me to do what an older brother should do when his baby brother's hurting.

"You right," I said. "Ricky should've zigzagged."

I flicked a rock that skipped five times. I gestured at Jay to see if he was watching or too busy debating how he'd knock me out this time.

"How you do that?" Jay tried another round rock without even giving me a chance to show him.

"Like this." I picked a flat rock for him to study. I wasn't ready to switch subjects, but it'd become easier just to let it ride like this. I took my arm back and whipped it, the rock skipping farther than the first time.

Jay nodded his head, picked a rock, and flicked. The stone made one big plunk into the water.

We both acted like all this was just a normal day and weren't about to throw punches five minutes ago. And even looking at Jay who started this, he didn't even seem upset, which meant he was still thinking about

Ricky, but I knew was also just code for Dad. Why he was upset. Why I was letting him get away with messing up my J's. But if we brought that up, then we'd have to bring up all the questions that had been floating. Like, why didn't Dad tell us he was sick? Why didn't Dad ever go to the doctor regularly? And most important, why didn't we get a chance to say goodbye? The list of whys and what ifs grew between us too. Including, would things have been different if Dad wouldn't have fled Compton in the first place? Did that move change the course of our lives? Shorten his? Dad would understand why we were ditching today. It was him that used to force us to go fishing with him. Take up hiking, and camping, being one with nature because it was so much different than the concrete blocks he grew up in.

Boyz n the Hood meant more to us than just another movie. It was our way of trying to understand where Dad was from. We filled in all the gaps he wouldn't talk about with moments from the movie. So much so it felt like everyone was real to us. Like these were Dad's neighbors growing up. Like we had an Uncle Doughboy and an Uncle Ricky. Jay and I talked about Compton so much you would've thought we were raised there. But like, the Compton of 1980 and not 2023. Jay and I being from Oregon, we always tried to find ways of qualifying where we were *really* from. Mainly because you get tired of people being surprised there were Black people living in Oregon or stating we weren't Black enough. I was embarrassed to say our Blackness used to mean to us we had to try and be what we thought white folks thought Black folks were. So, it became easier to pretend we weren't really from here, we just took on Dad's story. We talked about it so much our dad finally took us to visit Compton. I swear to God we were hype right until the moment we hit Grandma's block and then we just looked terrified. Like legit we thought a low rider was gonna swoop in and do a drive by like they did Ricky.

And even though we knew for a fact we'd be zigzagging all over the place, that didn't mean we wanted to test our theory.

That first night Jay and I slept on the floor. We'd watched way too many shows about kids getting hit from a stray bullet. It took about two nights for us to realize there would be no stray bullets. No crazy scenes like *Boyz n the Hood*, and Compton was just another regular neighborhood that we let the media work up our imagination about. Our fear of our own people. People we wanted to be close to but didn't know how.

I shoved Jay playfully, just to get him to loosen up. He gave me a head nod that I thought meant he was okay. Maybe embarrassed. Maybe really thinking about Ricky. I went to speak but I was interrupted by a deep voice calling in our direction. A white guy in his forties with the same two young boys who scared the deer trailing behind him. My stomach did a little flip-flop because I knew what was coming.

"This isn't a place for rough housing or fights." He had his hands on his hips.

I scanned him for any kind of sign he had some type of authority here. Like a park ranger. But he looked about as plain as anybody we'd see out on the river and walking the trails. I gave it a few seconds, mulling over how to respond. There's three common ways I'd always been received in Oregon. Token. Invisible. Or Suspect. His tone was condescending and rude so that just left the third. I looked over at Jay. At this point, I didn't know how he'd respond. His fuse was so short with me, who knew what might set him off. But Jay acted like he didn't even hear the man.

"I'm talking to you. Shouldn't you be in school?"

Jay whipped his head in the guy's direction. I was ready to curse him out, too. But when I looked at Jay. Thought about Dad. Thought about his absence. It loaded a sense of responsibility I never wanted to take ownership of before.

"Come on." I tapped Jay's arm. "Today's not the day for either of us."

We walked off, and the guy acted all accomplished as he got back to his kids. Then we found our trail. We usually looped around past the bike path that'd been overtaken not only by overgrown blackberry bushes but cleared out spaces for houseless people staying in small tents.

When we were a good distance away, I said, "This area goes on for miles and miles, but he wants to come where we are." I shook my head.

"Entitled." Jay smirked. "Probably thinks he's the only one paying taxes, and it's his land."

"Manifest destiny asshole."

"Oregon Trail loving colonizer."

"Policing with no badge." We riffed back and forth, saying all the things we wouldn't have courage to say to him if he was standing right in front of us.

"We could've stayed," Jay finally said.

I didn't answer him. We both knew why we left.

We climbed up the trail, hiking up a small climb so we could come back around and head home. The sky was partially cloudy, blues, purples, and pinks. When we reached the peak of the climb, we stood shoulder to shoulder like we'd summited Mount Kilimanjaro. We were in the thick of trees so green we couldn't even hear the traffic not too far away from us. The green spanned for miles, water running in between the other side of green trees that matched our side.

Dad would've loved seeing this. Jay had a nostalgic look in his eye, too. We watched a little bit longer until we knew it was time to head back. We wound down the hill, feet digging into the ground, so we stayed steady. Halfway down I finally got the courage to say,

"You thinking about Dad?"

I didn't stare at him, giving him the time to answer as I picked through rocks until I found another flat one, cold and smooth to the touch. I ran my thumb over it a few times, weighing it with my hands, then pocketing it for when we got close to the water.

"Yeah," Jay said. "But I don't wanna be sad right now. I just want to laugh. Be mad. Be bored. Anything but sad. I'll save that for tomorrow."

I gulped, that ache coming back. Dad's service, tomorrow. His ashes coming home to us, and part of his wishes were to be spread out somewhere in the open air. We both knew what that meant, that anytime we came out here we would only be thinking about Dad being gone. It had become some place different for us. Forever changed.

"Tomorrow," I agreed. "Now let me show you how to skip rocks."

Jay nodded, but didn't speak as we got closer to the base of the trail that led back to the riverbank.

Our silence was taken over by the same kids from earlier, coming close alongside us at lightning speed. We hopped onto the dirt off the trail to let them pass. The youngest face was beat red with a stick in his hand, running back and forth trying to catch his brother.

"That's my truck. Give it back." His little feet slapped the ground as he hightailed it to catch up to his brother.

I looked around, waiting on Mr. Serenity to give a tongue lashing like he did us, but he was nowhere to be found.

"Gary, you see their dad anywhere?"

"Nah," I said, looking out.

The older kid, like seven or eight, made his way to the water, brother following.

"Ah, damn." My chest hurt as obligation stirred inside me. I looked at Jay, and he shrugged, already knowing what I was thinking, already down for whatever I decided.

I started walking back toward where we first ran into the family to at least be a little closer to the water in case they needed help.

Jay hesitated. "You sure this is a good idea?"

"Probably not." My neck tensed, my eyes scanning in hyper alert watch.

A hundred yards out, we saw the dad running toward his boys, frantic because it was clear he'd lost them. And as soon as they were safe in his sight, he realized just like we did that the oldest was treading too far into the water. His little legs were wobbling beneath him as he slapped the truck around, teasing. The little one tugged on his brother, and I could see him slipping. The dad wouldn't make it in time. In an instant, I leapt to the water, no longer caring about my Jordans, and swooped up the boy just as he was about to go down. With my other hand, I grabbed his brother who was still hollering—crying about his truck now floating down the Willamette, for which I did not intend to risk my life to get. Their dad ran toward us, and immediately I flinched. Jay's body also shaking.

"He was … going down," I stammered.

The dad didn't speak. Just grabbed a hold of his kid, checking if he was okay. I knew the look. One that went quickly from securing safety to scolding for recklessness.

The older kid, knowing he was in big trouble, started crying about almost drowning. Their voices echoed across the water. I looked at the man and invoked my dad, proud of what I did, daring this man to say something. But he didn't. He just nodded a thanks and carried his kid to land.

I jogged over to Jay, who was shaking his head.

"He couldn't even say the words thank you," Jay said.

I chuckled, shaking off the fear that encroached my body. When we were at a safe distance, I gestured at the man berating us earlier.

The day ran through my mind, forcing the hard not to take everything over. "Look at him," I said.

Jay looked over. Then at me. I released a sly smile and without skipping a beat, Jay and I said in our best Doughboy voice, "Now keep them babies out the street!"

Then we busted out laughing as we ran in the other direction, Compton a million miles away and yet so close on the backdrop of Oregon pine trees by the hiking trails off the Willamette River.

ANIOMALLIA

Brynne Rebele-Henry

SOME NIGHTS IN THE ATTIC when the stillness around us gets too big, we hang up our blankets to make the shape of a planet in the shadows on the walls. We call the planet Aniomallia, and it is beautiful. Aniomallia has twelve people living in it, three cows, a cat, four dogs, eight birds, and a pony who sometimes passes through town on his way back from the circus. We lace our fingers together and make houses out of old cardboard boxes. The light from the gas lamp casts yellow stains on the plaster that we pretend are the moons. Aniomallia has five, plus twelve stars that surround the moons in yellow light. We have placed the boxes around the bed to make our own fortress. To get in, you have to crawl through the cardboard tunnels we have linked together to form a maze. Aniomallians speak what sounds like English but backwards. Sometimes our words get lost, and we end up tracing out the letters with a fingertip on each other's backs so as not to offend the Aniomallians with our English.

I once asked Lily, "Are we Aniomallians?" and she shook her head and said that to truly be Aniomallians, we would have to be unable to live anywhere else.

"So, we're adaptable?" "Yes," she said, "Like the camels from the Ark."

Our mothers used to sit us at the kitchen table with a Bible and squares of dehydrated jam. We'd gnaw on them while we memorized the passages they had bookmarked with pieces of dried plaited grass. Our favorite passage was the one about Gabriel and his wings.

Lily is five years older than me and remembers the outside world. She says that there are things called cars that you ride like horses and traffic is scary and the people wear rough blue pants called jeans and listen to something called an iPod that plays music like a hymn but different. Now, at fourteen, I try to remember the normal world, the place outside the compound, but I can't. Sometimes, at night, I'll make up stories about the things I remember, and I know Lily doesn't believe me, but she laughs anyway, tells me about all of the things we will never again see.

Our parents said they always knew Mr. B, but Lily says he just appeared one day, and they left behind everything they had, then came here with him in the middle of the night. Lily said she had been walking around their neighborhood trying to scuff the shine from her new shoes, putting off her math homework, and when she walked into the front hall, they were waiting.

Downstairs, our parents, Mr. B, and the girls argue, and we can hear the scrape of wooden spoons against plates. The girls are tall and always a little nervous. Sometimes they try to talk to us, ask us if there is a way out of the compound, but we don't know the answers, so we steal scraps from the kitchen and leave them on the pine tree stumps near the third house, where Mr. B keeps them.

Mr. B lives in the second house next to ours, but he's at ours more than his own and eats every meal with his hands held together in prayer while our fathers and mothers spoon soup mixed with rice into his mouth. Mr. B wears long white robes and has a beard down to his belly. The girls change every few months. Lily's mother says that's because they've gone to heaven after they passed the test of being Mr. B's wives. To be Mr. B's wife, you have to be good, he says. You have to pray for forty hours before the wedding, then you have to wear a crown made out of daisies and a wool robe, no matter what the season. He says you have to be able to recite the first Corinthians, and your heart has to be pure.

Our mothers and fathers and their sisters live below us in the main house. Their sisters aren't actually their sisters, just the girls who stay with our mothers and fathers. They put us here a while ago after Lily had invited one of the girls back with us. She had blue hair, a color we'd never seen on a person before. She was laughing when Mr. B came in and asked what was going on. Then she pulled a kitchen knife out of the drawer and tried to get him with it. Our mother said she just wasn't cut out for heaven, but Lily looked at me and said, in Aniomallian, that she just wasn't meant for here, and I agreed. The girl had a metal device with a voice coming out of it. Lily called the square a cellphone. The girl said she was calling the police, that this wasn't the summer camp she thought it was. Mr. B said she needed to repent and put her in the hut they keep in the yard for the ones who don't have enough God. Not girls like us. But then, one morning, he went to open the box and let her out, but she was gone. We were watching through the window and Lily said something in Aniomallian under her breath I didn't understand.

Mr. B says that when we're old enough, we won't need the same tests. We'll just ascend. We will wear dresses made out of burlap and strung with daisies and we will marry him and live in the bedroom in the house next to our parents for fourteen days. On the fourteenth day, we will eat a comb of honey each and drink the tea he brews, and we will go to heaven.

Sometimes Mr. B comes up to see us. He says to pretend to be asleep while he watches, and my eyelids flicker. He brings us maple leaves and tells us one of the mothers just had a baby, or that our fathers' new sister died, or that there is a new girl. Sometimes he brushes the knots out of my hair and then braids it into one long plait, and I have to try not to cry because he brushes so hard, I think my scalp is going to come off. The braid is so tight I think my eyeballs are being squeezed out. Lily closes her eyes when he does hers, sometimes she squeezes my wrist. Even after he leaves, we don't take them out.

When he arrives today, Mr. B says that before the compound, our mothers lived in sin and our fathers in disgrace—bastards without a calling. He says that outside of the compound there is a world full of heathens who want to take virtue from us. He says they don't even have a God they believe in. He says that this way, we are best, that we will be pure and wholesome and blessed in his eyes. Mr. B says he loves our mothers, too, anyway. Their hands are always raw and red, the skin chapped. This is all we know, really, about our mothers.

They long ago stopped talking to us, then they stopped talking at all, and now they just nod when they bring our food up to the attic. They used to teach us how to make butter, how to knead bread, how to speak and recite scriptures, but after they brought us up here, everything stopped. They said it was for our purity, that one of the girls and our own desires had contaminated us, and we needed to purge so when we come out, God will take us by the hand, and we'll learn the way up to heaven.

We hear his steps down, the ladder hitting the floor again. When we're sure he's gone, Lily brushes the crown of my hair loose with her fingers and whispers in Aniomallian: "Silly man." Her face is tight.

I say, "In Aniomallia, there is no marriage, and you never need to brush your hair because it's always perfect. In Aniomallia, you don't get married, and you don't die or go to heaven, you just grow wings when you get too old, then fly somewhere else."

Lily smiles and says something that doesn't make sense. "It's not like that in the real world, either."

"Where else is there besides here and Aniomallia?" I ask.

"Outside," she says.

I just nod, touch the goose bumps covering my arms.

Lily sees them, then says, "The girls in our favorite Aniomallian neighborhood are replacing the church with a dress shop, and the cat with the one green eye gave birth to three kittens. Except in Aniomallia, there isn't any birth, the babies just appear out of thin air." She says there isn't any bleeding either, that you never really become a woman in Aniomallia.

Earlier today, Mr. B said that when I have my first blood soon, that the two of us will marry him, and then we will marry God, and then I will ascend. He said he'd kept Lily up here for too long to take care of me, that she's had to wait too much.

Now, Lily takes the hairbrush and starts sliding it under the attic window.

"What are you doing?"

"We won't have to go through with it," Lily says.

"Go through with what?"

"Marrying him."

The window springs loose with a sharp sound and Lily sighs, then looks around nervously. She says I don't understand what's going on, that I couldn't know what she has to do. She says she's going to get out when she can and take me too. I don't know what to say to this, so I hum to myself in the language that belongs to both of us.

We hear the clink of the attic door unlocking, and my mother slides three paper plates into the room that contain: two pieces of chicken, two pieces of bread, and one carrot. A cup of grape juice. A bottle of water. Two paper cups. Mr. B says we are here so that when we start to bleed, we'll be pure for him.

Lily says, "I had to stay up here because of the girl with blue hair."

"Do you mean because she got a knife?" I ask.

"Because of the way I looked at her."

"What do you mean, *looked*?"

"You know, looked."

I nod but I don't know. She says she's never wanted to be a wife, and I say I already knew that. She says I don't know what she meant by that.

Last week, when I woke up to a red stain on my underwear, I started stuffing my underwear with paper towels she'd saved from our meals. I didn't want to be like the girls outside, in the third house. The cramps hurt, but Lily said everything hurts, and having to be a wife and drink a cup of the honey tea that Mr. B brews would hurt more.

Lily says that she thinks she is abnormal, that she kissed that blue-haired girl in the woods when she first arrived, that she liked it, so she helped her escape. She says that the girl came here at first because her parents thought it was a Bible summer camp, but after they kissed the first time, and the girl was led into the third house, she realized it wasn't.

We eat the food that our mothers brought earlier—it's stale, mold spatters the corners of the bread slices. I try to tell Lily there is mildew on our pieces, but she's muttering to herself and using her plastic dinner fork to wiggle the screen loose. It's rusty and squeaks every time she tries to open it. She says to start singing hymns so they won't notice. I start singing. She gets the screen loose and it comes away with a creak.

She closes the window and says to pretend that nothing happened and hopefully they won't notice.

Downstairs, the screen door bangs as they head to tonight's sermon. It's dark and humid and the air hisses with cicadas. Lily pushes the loose screen out of the window, and it falls onto the grass. It is about fifteen feet down. She has to squeeze to get out of the window, and she drops silently down, rolls on the grass. She motions for me to come down, and I put one leg out, then the other, and jump. My ankle twinges. It hurts when I stand up.

Lily smiles. She grabs my hand, and we creep through the little garden, past the barn and second house. We reach the woods. There is no fence, just barbed wire wrapped around the trees. I try to climb through, but the wire catches on my skin, and I feel blood running down my legs. I get the wire off my leg and crawl out. The air is different now, shiny, and warm. I look back at Aniomallia, and we start to run. In the distance the girls scream hymns. Their voices turn the air sour.

LAST DANCE (ABOVE WATER)

Madelin A. Medina

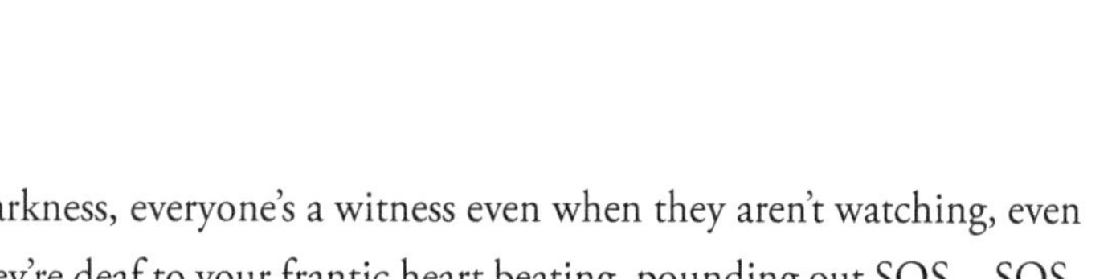

In the darkness, everyone's a witness even when they aren't watching, even when they're deaf to your frantic heart beating, pounding out SOS…SOS… SOS…while you're drowning in the bass of blaring music, while your primo's hand, at your waist, leads you where he wants you, and you feel his soft parts growing hard against you.

You're a woman, now,

he shouts, but it's a clammy whisper breathed into your ear, says your name and it's like a dirty word bc you're 15 and your serpent body won't stop betraying you, bc ever since you started bleeding she's been your worst frenemy—smile like a switchblade, liking your posts but leaving encrypted comments to decipher.

Lo provocaste y a veces eso pasa. Olvídalo,[1]

---

1 Translation: You provoked him and sometimes that happens. Forget it.

Mami says, but instead you cut biology to cry in the school bathroom that no one uses, locking yourself in a stall in case someone walks in and finds you, bc you don't want to be another girl they'll start a rumor about, you're already the girl choking on her shame despite being believed, trying to save face by keeping her head above water.

A BEAUTIFUL PARADOX

Kate Larkindale

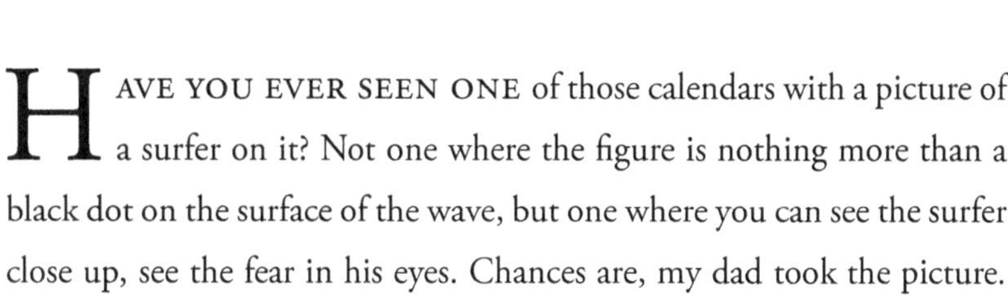

HAVE YOU EVER SEEN ONE of those calendars with a picture of a surfer on it? Not one where the figure is nothing more than a black dot on the surface of the wave, but one where you can see the surfer close up, see the fear in his eyes. Chances are, my dad took the picture. Look at the bottom and you'll see his name, Gary Weston, known to everyone in the surfing community as Gazza or Gaz.

His van pulls up in front of Mum's house just after five. I've been up for an hour, eyes fixed on the front window, waiting for him. I'm out the front door before the van has even stopped, my feet barely touching the dew-drenched lawn as I run.

"Dad!" I call, wading through the thick black exhaust that belches from the back of the ancient panel van.

"Kai!" His head pops out the driver's side window, blond and shaggy as ever, his face creased into a white-toothed grin. "Hop in, mate."

The van, affectionately known as Sheila, is loaded to the gunnels as usual. Dad tends to live out of her when he's in Australia and I don't blame him; the apartment he rents in St. Kilda is not home. I move a couple of camera bags, a pillow and three paperback westerns off the passenger seat before swinging myself into it.

"How was Hawaii?" I ask as Dad pulls away from the curb, backfiring twice on the way out of the cul-de-sac.

"It was good, Kai," he says, the aquamarine eyes he branded me with turning my way. "I got some great shots, and the waves were bonza! I missed you, though. Next time we'll have to see if your mother will let you come with me."

"Fat chance," I mutter. If it involves Dad, my mother is wary. If it involves missing school *and* Dad, there'd be a better chance of finding an ice cream parlor in Hell. How they managed to stay together twelve years is beyond me.

"How is she, anyway?" Dad looks sideways at me, flooring the accelerator as we turn onto the motorway. Sheila rattles and groans as if she's going to fall apart before settling into a low growl that makes the floor vibrate through my feet.

"She's Mum," I say with a shrug. "You know…."

"Yeah, I know." The smile he tosses me is sad, a twist to the corner of his mouth that speaks volumes. He turns the radio on and fiddles with the dial as he searches for something he likes, finally settling on an oldies station playing something by the Stones. I groan, reaching out to change it but my hand is slapped away before I get close. I wait until he's not looking, humming as he drives one-handed down the road, and spin the dial, finding something more appropriate for a fifteen-year-old to listen to.

"Don't you touch that," Dad warns, cutting off Tame Impala and bringing back the Stones.

The sun is climbing in the sky as we turn off at Jan Juc. The ocean spreads into the distance, blue and infinite. I watch my father's shoulders relax, the tension in his face smoothing out with the balm of open sea. I wind down the window and breathe the tang of salt. Dad slows Sheila as we climb the road to the top of the cliffs. Snakes and butterflies are battling it out somewhere in my midsection, and when I look at my hands, I'm not surprised to see them trembling a little.

The car park above the cove is almost full of rusting station wagons and old vans like Sheila. The odd SUV or sedan is conspicuous, advertising tourists.

Dad grins at me as he slides out of the van. "You ready, mate?"

"I guess…."

We walk the cliff-top track slowly, studying the waves that pound the sand below. They're towering, the sound they make as they hurtle towards the beach audible even from here. The creatures in my belly scramble faster now, and for a moment I think I might lose my breakfast. But I haven't eaten any breakfast.

"You like them down there?" Dad asks, pointing to the waves in the cove. "They're big, but they're pretty predictable. You see? Always the third in the set."

I study the sea, wanting to be able to see what he sees. Then he starts walking again, heading further along the cliff top, and leaving the cove below.

"Where are we going?" I ask, in a sudden panic that he's not going to let me surf it, that he's changed his mind.

"We're going around the Button," he tells me. "I want to see how she looks over at Winkipop." I look down at the rocky outcrop that separates Bell's Beach from the next bay. Despite being right next to each other, depending on the wind, the surf can be different on each side.

"What do you think?" Dad squints at me in the sunlight, his weather-beaten face creased like soft leather. "You like it better here, or at Bell's?"

"Bell's," I say, not seeing much difference between the two. The waves are terrifying at both. I watch a surfer take off, speeding down the face of a wave, keeping low to begin with, then flying up the surface, too high. I lose sight of him as he's caught in the crest, the wave taking him down with it as it hurls itself into the shore.

"Righto, then." Dad grins, boyish again. "Let's get our gear out."

Standing on the packed wet sand, I can feel the force of the waves pounding in as well as hear it. They'd looked big from the cliff top, but down here, they are gargantuan. I've been surfing since I could stand, pretty much, but never here. Dad's been priming me for years, each new beach a test to pass. The prize? Bell's. But now that I'm here, I'm not so sure I'm ready.

As I squirm into my wetsuit, I listen to the surfers around us, trying to glean a hint about how to tackle this surf. I'm not sure I can even paddle out to the break it's so big. But my father seems unconcerned, peering through his camera lens.

"Crikey!" exclaims the man next to me. "She's a killer today."

"Tell me about it!" comes the reply. "Look at me board!" I turn, trying not to look like I've been eavesdropping, and catch sight of the board, snapped in two.

"Strewth, mate!" laughs the first man, clapping his friend on the shoulder. "I'd better get you a cold one. You look like you need it!" As they pass us, one of them turns and sees Dad.

"Gazza?" he asks, already moving toward him, hand outstretched. "Saw the pictures from the Classic. They're unbelievable!"

"Thanks." Dad looks up and shakes the surfer's hand. "How is it out there?"

"She's tough," the second surfer says, holding out the broken board. "Would you mind signing it? Not much good for anything else now…."

Dad laughs and reaches into his bag for a Sharpie. As he signs the board, the first surfer catches sight of me.

"This your sprog, Gaz?"

"Yeah." Dad tosses me a lazy smile. "This is my son, Kai."

"Hey, Kai." The second surfer retrieves his busted board and studies the signature scrawled across it. "You're surfing this?"

"Yeah." I nod, enjoying their surprise, watching as they turn to Dad for the truth.

"Kai's been working for this," Dad tells them. "How long would you say, Kai?"

"All my life." And it's the truth.

The surfer with the splintered board shakes his head, exchanging a glance with his friend before heading back up the beach. "Good luck."

"Ready?" Dad has his camera slung around his neck, his board under one arm.

"Uh…sure," I say, watching the two surfers throw themselves down on a blanket in the dunes, their Esky already open to reveal rows of VBs on ice.

"You don't have to, Kai," Dad says, his eyes boring into mine. "I know you can do this, but if you don't think you can, we can save it. Bell's won't be going anywhere."

"I can!" I protest, zipping my wetsuit and picking my board up off the sand.

"Let's do it, then!"

I run down the beach after Dad, the sand warm against the soles of my feet, cooling as we get close to the sea. I shiver as the water races up the beach, covering my feet before scurrying back across the sand.

"We'll paddle out that way," Dad says, pointing toward a group of black dots bobbing on the water beyond the fury of the waves. "Stay low, and go with the flow, okay?"

"Okay."

I start paddling, following close on my father's heels, but not so close that I'll get a board between the eyes if he gets washed back toward me. It feels as if I'm making no progress, the waves' strength too much for my arms to contest. Diving beneath the surging water, my arms scoop as fast as they can. It surprises me when I look back at the beach and find it so far away, the people little more than matchstick silhouettes against the yellow sand. I duck beneath the ocean again, and when I come up, I'm there. Searching for Dad, I find him sitting on his board a few feet away. He looks calm, the camera in his hands already. I paddle over, exhausted by my assault on the sea.

"You made it!" Dad grins at me as I clamber, panting, onto my board. "Just let me know when you're going to take off, okay? I don't want to miss you." He pats the camera.

"I'll take a break first," I manage, chest still heaving from the effort of getting out here. No wonder these guys wait for the perfect wave.

I let the sun warm me as I sit on my board, the swell rising and falling beneath me. I watch other guys in the lineup take waves, some making it all the way in, others giving up early on, popping out the back of the wave and sliding back into the lineup again. I can hear the click of Dad's camera as he shoots. Gulls swoop and dive, screaming at us from on high. I breathe deeply, the salt air so fresh it almost hurts my lungs. I feel at peace here. Nothing matters except the waves, making their endless journey to the shore.

Once my limbs have stopped trembling and my breathing is regular again, I start watching the waves, searching for the one I'm going to ride.

I study them, trying to understand the rhythm of each set the way Dad seems to. It is not long before I see it coming, the one I want to take.

"Now!" I yell as I throw myself down on the board and start paddling in. I can't check to see if Dad's heard me, so just trust that he has, glancing over my shoulder every second or so to see if it's time to get up on my feet. The wave forms behind me, curling upwards, huge and capped with white foam. I push myself up with all the strength in my arms and shoulders, gathering my feet beneath me, hoping, praying that I won't slip or lose my balance.

I'm there.

I crouch low, knees bent, the front of my board at the perfect angle as I race across the glassy surface of the wave. I'm speeding, flying through this. My heart pounds in my chest, not with exertion this time, but with the pure joy of this ride. The wave tries to fling me upwards, into the frothy cap at the top, but I push the nose of the board down, keeping in at the base just the way Dad taught me to.

And then I see him. He's on his own board, standing, camera in front of his face as if he were on the sand, not this unpredictable slice of ocean. I'm racing toward him, the board pointed directly at the camera lens, directly between his eyes. If I keep going, I'm going to plough into him. I'm going to drive the board right into his skull.

I don't move.

I try to make my legs work, try to shift the board up the wave at least a little, but they won't obey me. My heart flies into my throat, choking me. I'm going to kill Dad. A secret stab of excitement slices through me at the thought. I could do it. I could take a life. Not just any life either: my father's life. I wonder why this thought is not frightening. This idea should be horrifying, not alluring.

Move! My mind cries out, my eyes fixed on the spot where the board is going to make contact. Move, you idiot! I'm not sure who I'm thinking this at, him or myself.

I'm past him. At the last possible second he rocks his hips and slides out of my way as I shoot by. I turn my head, checking that he's okay, and in that brief second my weight shifts, the board points its nose toward the top of the curling wave and I find myself shooting up the face. I try desperately to get down again, but it is too late. The momentary loss of focus is enough.

The next thing I know I'm falling. My feet are no longer on the board although I can feel it dragging behind me by its tether. The wave hurls me into the ocean, surges over me. I'm dragged along the bottom for a while, coarse sand filling my mouth and nose. I can't see, can't breathe, can't even figure out where the sky might be. I struggle against the force. My hands claw at water until one breaks the surface. I pop up, gasping for air, only to be smashed back down by the force of another wave. I feel the board tear free of my ankle, a sudden lightness that brings little comfort.

When I surface again, eyes burning with salt, I search for the shore. I know I need to let the sea carry me there. Before I manage to find it, I'm crushed under again, saltwater filling my mouth and nose. Something slams into my upper arm, which is painful at first then grows numb and heavy. I don't know if I'm moving it, just scrabble with the other hand, feeling my strength draining from me with each new assault by the ocean.

I come up again, dumped down the next second. My arm twists behind me as I'm tossed through the sandy seabed. For a moment the pain is monumental. I'm sure my arm has been torn off, that it is floating through the water, no longer attached to my body. Somehow, though, this thought is not as horrifying as it should be. I stop fighting, allow the waves to toss me back and forth, tumble me as if I were a pair of socks in a dryer. The cold water cradles me, rocking me like a baby.

I feel heat on my face, sunlight making my eyelids glow red. From a long way away, I can hear someone calling my name.

"Kai!" The voice is insistent. "Kai! Listen to me, Kai!" I push my eyelids up, a difficult chore, and find Dad leaning over me.

"You're okay, mate," he tells me, relief painted across his features. "Just lie still." I nod, barely able to move my head. I'm so tired. I wonder if I'll ever be able to move again. I try to raise my left arm, but find I can't and wonder if it is still out there, floating amongst the vicious waves with whatever is left of my surfboard.

FOUR DAYS LATER I LIMP back into my house, leaning heavily on Dad's arm. My left arm is in a sling—not ripped off, but it might as well have been. At least, that's what the surgeon told me. He'd never seen a shoulder so badly dislocated, ligaments and muscles torn around the displaced bone. Dad pushes open the door to my bedroom.

"There you are, mate." Dad gestures at the wall behind my bed where a series of photographs have been mounted, new additions to the ones that have hung there for years. Poster sized, the colors are so vibrant the pictures seem to almost pour off the wall. I step forward, studying them.

In the first, I'm crouching, just up on the board, low on the wave as I get my balance. I can see the uncertainty on my face, that moment when I was praying to be sure-footed. In the second, I'm upright, arms out, regal. I look triumphant, exhilarated, as I speed across the surface of the wave. In the third, I'm on top of the camera. I can see the murderous abandon in my eyes, the reflection of the cameraman, Dad, in my glossy black pupil. I can see the poison there, the rage. The last picture shows me tumbling, the board and me two separate things now. My body has lost its grace, is all angles as I crash into the surging foam below.

Underneath each picture is written, "The Beautiful Paradox." I turn to Dad. His hand is huge and warm on my uninjured shoulder.

"The ocean, mate," he says, reaching out to trace the letters with his fingers. "She's gorgeous, but you can't forget, she's savage too. But I think you know that, don't you?"

I do, but I can't help thinking those words mean more to him than what he's said. I look at my face in the third photograph and know they mean more to me. It's not just the sea that can be savage; loving someone can be too.

ARTEMIS//APOLLO

Christina Polge

it is like

she is the name whispered into my
pillow when i am making wishes on
stars that don't know who i am. she
is the fingertips on my spine and the
lips against my ear and the dancing
she is always dancing across my mind since
i am always thinking about holding her—
gentle and tight and dreamy—and i realize

he is the name on the tip of my
tongue, i find myself working it
into the conversation whenever i can,
he is the song in my head when i
am trying to memorize anything else
and he just keeps singing until i
think about kissing him—fast and
messy and real—and i realize that

good lord

it would fix me

it would break me

OUR CORRESPONDENCE

Maia Cataldo

Monday, October 3
2:23p.m.

Hello Eric!

Mrs. Hart assigned partners today in class and put us together. We are supposed to read one of the books on the list (attached) and either write a joint paper on it or give a ten minute presentation. I think Mrs. Hart is sending you the assignment, but I'll attach it here in case! I think a presentation would be pretty interesting, but I guess we should pick a book first.

I am leaning towards Villette by Charlotte Brontë but I understand if you don't want to read it. Though I do think you should at least consider it.

Anyways, let me know what you think. I hope you feel better soon!

Thanks!
Beth

(PS even if you're planning on coming to school tomorrow I would still appreciate a reply so I can begin planning tonight. Thanks)

Monday, October 3
8:40p.m.

Beth

paper's easier. I googled Villette and don't love the sound of "drawn into adventure and romance"... what about Catch 22?

I won't be in school tomorrow

Eric

Tuesday, October 4
2:34p.m.

Hello Eric,

I'm fine with the paper option. In regards to *Catch 22*, I'm thoroughly bored of reading war texts. Furthermore I feel that books like *Catch 22* one could be motivated to read on their own, but perhaps we should seize the opportunity to utilize school as a motivational tool to help us read more challenging texts. I actually think you might like *Villette* in all honesty. Also if you're still sick, I don't want to get stuck doing this project mostly by myself, reading a book I have no passion for. Plus…we had to choose today and *Catch 22* was the first to go, so… *Villette* won't be that bad, I promise! I am happy to shoulder most of the brunt work seeing as I got my first pick.

Thanks!
Beth

Tuesday, October 4
3:06p.m.

Beth

Lol there's no movie version of Villette I looked

E

Tuesday, October 4
3:09p.m.

Eric -

You don't need to pretend you're stupid, I am not sharing our correspondence with the class you know. Let me know if you need help acquiring the text.

Beth

Tuesday, October 4
3:17p.m.

U don't have to call this a "correspondence" when I'm not showing these to the class either

Tuesday, October 4
3:22p.m.

Eric,

How far are you in the book?

Beth

Tuesday, October 4
7:20p.m.

don't have it yet

Tuesday, October 4
7:27p.m.

Eric,

What is your address I can drop off a copy tonight. The sooner we read it the sooner we can begin writing.

Beth

Tuesday, October 4
7:35p.m.

Beth

im getting one tomorrow

thanks
Eric

Tuesday, October 4
8:01p.m.

Eric

I left the book on your porch. Please start reading tonight! The paper is due in 2 weeks!

Best,
Beth

Tuesday, October 4
8:58p.m.

how did you get my address?? im a fast reader, already past the part where she lives with her godmother. Lucy's on the way to Villette, boring so far. tell me it gets better

Tuesday, October 4
9:06p.m.

Eric,

The internet. Also I kind of remembered our bus route in the fifth grade. I'm glad it landed in the right hands.

Congratulations on your quick reading skills, but I warn you using SparkNotes is not going to be sufficient for our paper. I intend on getting an A. It's imperative to have good grades this semester, it's the last one colleges will see. Speaking of, when are you coming back to school? Are you really very ill? Isn't soccer almost over? Are you missing it? I thought you were applying to Brown for soccer?

The book does get better, it gets really good actually. Lucy is a very interesting and funny character, I think you will like her interactions with Dr John.

If I don't respond it's because I'm going to bed shortly.
Beth

Tuesday, October 4
9:15p.m.

Beth

5th grade bus route?? jeez. im sure we'll get an A, Mrs. H is afraid of you. I might come friday. How did u know about Brown??

the team seems to be fine without me. you ask a lot of questions. this book is kind of depressing, not funny

wow early bedtime ok
E

Tuesday, October 4
9:42p.m.

Beth

ok ur right, the whole dance part is kind of funny—esp the part where Dr John gets mad at Ginevra for being a bitch to his mom. he's such a mamma's boy

Tuesday, October 4
10:38p.m.

Beth

this french professor is such a dick. we're not supposed to like him, right?

Tuesday, October 4
11:24p.m.

Beth

Is Lucy in love with Dr John? You'd think we'd know cuz she talks to us like directly, it's confusing. I think that part is dumb

Wednesday, October 5
12:50a.m.

ok this is getting stressful. Is Polly going to steal Dr John away from Lucy cuz she's hot now? but isn't she like ten years younger than him? I can't read any more of this shit.

Wednesday, October 5
1:30a.m.

Dr John is engaged to Polly??? Lucy says she's happy for them? bs. she's hanging out with the asshole professor M. Paul guy more, but I thought she liked Dr John?? this is such a stupid book.

Wednesday, October 5
2:48a.m.

also, wtf is with the whole nun thing? is it a ghost or what?

Wednesday, October 5
3:09a.m.

oh shit it was Ginevra's boyfriend!? dude this is a scandalous book! this school girl was doing it with some older guy in the attic? who she ran away with cuz hes rich but he has no $$? Lucy was right to hate her. she's the worst.

but why would he dress up like a nun?

Wednesday, October 5
4:33a.m.

I get that Lucy and M. Paul professor guy are now in love, but he was such an asshole! She gets to run her own school cuz he like gave her $$ whatever but srsly what does she see in him

Wednesday, October 5
5:49a.m.

he DIES?!

so she's never actually happy then. what a fucked up book! great choice Beth. im so glad we read this shit instead of Catch 22.

im going to bed now.

Wednesday, October 5
7:04a.m.

Eric,

Good lord. You completely spoiled the ending for me! Not cool.

I'm sorry the book made you feel angry and confused and upset, but the fact that you stayed up all night to finish it shows that it *is* a great book. *And* that you clearly enjoyed reading it. So you're welcome! Lucy is a complex character and her life is not perfect, not all stories have happy endings.

Seeing as you finished the book first, you can get a head start on the paper once you wake up. I was thinking our focus could be on M. Paul and Lucy's relationship, how he is the only one who truly sees her for who she is. Maybe start pulling some quotes we can use.

I'm sorry you had such a rough night, but I won't lie I'm immensely relieved you have actually read the book in its entirety.

Sweet dreams.
Beth

Wednesday, October 5
1:34p.m.

Beth

I don't think that's true at all. no one got close to understanding her. The whole book, it was like Lucy was on the outside looking in. everyone has their own life, she never gets her own, even when she got to open that school. she doesn't get to be happy and everyone else is happy and in love and shit

which is why it's stupid

Eric

Wednesday, October 5
2:30p.m.

Eric,

What a brilliant idea for our thesis! "Lucy Snowe: Always on the outside looking in" (working title, of course). Let's start there.

Beth

Wednesday, October 5
2:36p.m.

ok i'll start pulling quotes about that

Wednesday, October 5
2:41p.m.

Eric

I just shared a document with you, add quotes/notes/etc. I'll be done reading tonight and then I'll start adding stuff. You're coming to school on Friday, right?

Beth

Wednesday, October 5
2:47p.m.

Beth

ok thanks. idk

Wednesday, October 5
2:55p.m.

Eric,

I heard Jay saying you were in the hospital for awhile, did you get injured playing soccer?

Beth

Wednesday, October 5
2:58p.m.

no

Wednesday, October 5
3:21p.m.

Ginevra is the worst. She deserves that buffoon. I don't think M Paul is an asshole, but… Lucy could definitely do better.

Wednesday, October 5
4:05p.m.

Beth,

added some notes to the doc. im gonna start writing the 1st body paragraph about Lucy looking into/being on the outside of Dr John and Polly's relationship.

M. Paul acted like a dick at that dance they went to, and was so weird at apologizing for it! all im saying is I wasn't that put off when he died. and yeah, she totally could.

E

Thursday, October 6
4:46p.m.

Eric,

I am finally done reading. Your paragraph is great! I think add one more quote from the very beginning, she really was on the outside in those first couple chapters. But it's quite strong otherwise. I'll take the paragraph regarding Ginevra and De Hamal, we can both tackle the part about M. Paul and then tag team it on the intro and conclusion. If we finish early we can send it to Mrs. Hart for edits before we submit.

Beth

Thursday, October 6
5:01p.m.

Beth

you sure it's clear enough with our thesis? I can add more about her time at the school too, I think it's important to do other moments besides relationships. feel free to edit my grammar n stuff. I wont be butt hurt if you add in a comma or something

Eric

Thursday, October 6
5:12p.m.

Eric,

Really, your analysis is quite compelling. I think it ties very nicely to the thesis. I underestimated you, Eric, your writing is great. But add in whatever you think is necessary.
Since you'll be in class tomorrow, we can discuss how we want to shape the ending then.

See you tomorrow!
Beth

Thursday, October 6
5:40p.m.

Beth

im not coming to school tmrw. not up to it (or soccer) just going thru some shit rn

sorry
Eric

Thursday, October 6
5:45p.m.

Eric,

Oh okay. Is there anything I can do? Drop off assignments or materials or something? I can collect stuff from your teachers and run them by tomorrow, just let me know. And if you need to take a step back from the paper don't worry about it.

Are you still going to college? Sorry if that's a stupid question…

Best,
Beth

Thursday, October 6
5:56p.m.

thanks. I get stuff emailed. school work's not the problem, I can do the paper. I promise we'll get an A and if we don't it won't be my fault ;) (that was a joke cuz obv u would never not get an A…)

Idk about college yet. I mean, im gonna go I just don't know if it's gonna be Brown or whatever

thanks for the help. and just keep this to urself plz

E

Thursday, October 6
5:57p.m.

Eric,

Of course. You have my strictest confidence.

Warmly,
Beth

Thursday, October 6
6:00p.m.

Ok no need to get all formal. I edited the paragraph, lmk what you think

Eric

Thursday, October 6
6:16p.m.

Sorry. It's great! I left a few comments, mainly small stuff. You can look over mine when you get the chance.

Beth

Thursday, October 6
6:24p.m.

Beth

I really like the quotes about Ginevra and De Hamal, your writing is great. Do you think our paragraphs will connect? I feel like my sentences are much simpler.. I can try to beef mine up if u think that might help

Thursday, October 6
6:32p.m.

Eric,

Thank you! I think part of what is interesting about a group paper is the different voices coming out. I like your part a lot, I wouldn't change it at all! Mrs. Hart said she wants to be able to hear our individual voices while reading, only the main ideas and analysis should align. I don't want to speak too soon, but I think this paper is going to kick ASS!

Beth

Thursday, October 6
6:38p.m.

Beth

haha okay then I won't change anything

PS i didn't think you were the kind of person who would use "ass" in a school email

Eric

Thursday, October 6
6:55p.m.

There's a lot you don't know about me then I guess!

:) Beth

Friday, October 7
2:33p.m.

Hey Eric!

I think we got a lot of good work done today in class! If we spend the weekend working on our prospective paragraphs, exchange some edits and start our intro/conclusion we should be good to send Mrs. Hart a draft on Monday! Let's touch base on Sunday night and see where we're at with it.

Glad to see you back in class :)
Beth

Friday, October 7
2:36p.m.

Hey Beth

it was good to be back :)

maybe we should work on it together this weekend since we missed so much time this week. U wanna meet in the library tmrw? Noon?

lmk
Eric

Friday, October 7
2:37p.m.

Hey Eric,

Tomorrow sounds great. I'll see you there :)

Beth

Sunday, October 9
8:11p.m.

Hey Beth

I'll be at school tmrw, but I was thinking maybe we should stay after and meet with Mrs. Hart about the paper? might be better to get in person edits rather than doc comments. then we could just go work on it in the library afterwards. We were more productive yesterday doing it that anyway. I just emailed Mrs. Hart, lmk if you would be down.

:) Eric

Sunday, October 9
8:13p.m.

Hey Eric,

I have a club meeting after school, but if you want to meet with Mrs. Hart I could meet you in the library afterwards!

PS thanks for confiding in me about all your "shit" yesterday. I mean I've never been hospitalized or anything, but I'm no stranger to panic attacks and the like… you aren't alone, you know?

Beth :)

Sunday, October 9
8:15p.m.

Great see you then!

and thanks :)
Eric

Tuesday, October 11
2:05p.m.

Hey Eric,

I noticed you weren't in school today…I feel like it's my fault. I'm sorry. I didn't mean to react so…quickly? It's not that I don't feel anything, I just wasn't expecting it, you, whatever. I'm not used to romantic gestures… I'm not sure what to do.

Anyways, the paper is almost done. I think all it needs is a once over and then we can submit it early, so that's good.

Anyways, sorry
Beth

Tuesday, October 11
2:15p.m.

Idk what I was thinking. sorry

I don't think it will be ready early. there's still a lot to do on the conclusion and stuff. I feel like it would be a mistake to submit it too early before we're done.

E

Tuesday, October 11
3:20p.m.

Eric

Don't worry about it. It's forgotten.

If you want to continue working on it, then we don't have to submit it early, I just thought it might be nice to take something off your plate.

I'll take another look at it tonight.
Beth

Tuesday, October 11
3:25p.m.

Beth

My plate is fine. I want this on my plate.

Eric

Tuesday, October 11
3:30p.m.

Okay, good.

Beth

Wednesday, October 12
2:31p.m.

Hey Beth,

that first line we were talking about today in class, I think I know how to solve the awkward-ness problem. I added it in a comment on the doc, lmk what you think. Also im going to start fixing up the ending.

Eric

Wednesday, October 13
2:40p.m.

Hey Eric,

Brilliant! I love it. I'm working on the bibliography now, I'll send it when I'm done for a once-over.

:)Beth

Wednesday, October 13
2:42p.m.

oh shit I forgot all about the bibliography! Sounds good.

Eric :)

Wednesday, October 13
3:06p.m.

Okay I shared the bibliography! I read over the comments you left and fixed anything glaring, but otherwise I think you're being paranoid. If we get too nitty gritty it will go south fast, trust me. I think we should polish what we can and then sleep on it before submitting. I think it's what Lucy Snowe would do.

Perhaps we should meet in the library tomorrow so we can read it over once more before submitting?

Beth :)

Wednesday, October 13
3:08p.m.

Yes great

Eric

Sunday, October 17
4:47p.m.

Hey Eric,

Did you see Mrs. Hart graded the paper? Quite fast, huh? I didn't want to open it yet without you.

Beth

Sunday, October 17
4:51p.m.

okay let's open it at 5:00p.m. EST exactly

PS I know it's good, but I'm starting to get nervous

Eric

Sunday, October 17
4:52p.m.

Yes me too. 5:00p.m. EST it is!

B

Sunday, October 17
5:01p.m.

A!!!!!!!!!!!!!!!!!!!!!!!!!!!!!!

Beth :)

Sunday, October 17
5:01p.m.

fuck yeah!!!

I've never had a teacher describe something I've written as "divinely eloquent" haha

:) Eric

Sunday, October 18
5:02p.m.

Eric,

I couldn't agree more with her.

It was truly a pleasure working with you. I would apologize for making you read something so out of your wheelhouse, but I think the A alone makes it worth it. (Don't think I won't forget how you stayed up all night enraptured by the words of Charlotte Bronte, either. So instead I'll just thank you for your artistic cooperation ;)).

And if you're still thinking about applying to college, I would submit this with my portfolio if I were you.

I hope to work with you again in the future.

Sincerely,
Beth

Sunday, October 18
5:05p.m.

Beth,

thank you. this book…surprised me. that's all I'm going to say about it. I had fun writing with you

and you were right, it is a kick ASS paper ;)

Best,
Eric

Wednesday, October 21
2:40p.m.

Hey Eric,

Mrs. Hart asked me if I would send you some notes from our lecture on *Heart of Darkness*, so I've attached them along with a few handouts from this week.
Also, I guess I just want to know how you are… Are you alright? I hope to see you back in school soon. Let me know if I can do anything.

Best,
Beth

Monday, October 26
2:32p.m.

Hey Eric,

Just checking to make sure you got those notes I sent you last week? We have a test on the first half of *Heart of Darkness* this

Wednesday. I mean I doubt you'll be forced to take it if you come in, but just thought I'd keep you in the loop.

I drove by your house yesterday idk why. Send me a signal if you're okay, okay?

Warmly,
Beth

Wednesday, October 27
2:27p.m.

Eric the test was so hard, if you need help preparing for it don't hesitate, seriously! It kicked my butt that's for sure, and you know me! It's not really important, but anyways…hope you're well.

Yours,
Beth

PS it's not something I did, is it?

Wednesday, October 27
4:33p.m.

Eric,

I also realize that we aren't actually "friends" so I will stop overstepping now, I'm sorry.

Beth

Wednesday, October 27
5:04p.m.

Hey Beth

I'm sorry ive been a little out of touch. i guess i kinda crashed again.. anyways im home now though and will be back soon probs. thanks for the notes!

And no, it's nothing u did

your friend,
Eric

Wednesday, October 27
4:37p.m.

I am ever so glad to hear it! I'm attaching more notes on what to study for the test, not that you have to worry about it right now! Just wanted you to have it before I forgot.

I'll see you soon?!
Beth

Friday, October 29
2:06p.m.

Hey Beth,

thanks for the notes, Mrs Hart said I did pretty good on the test today but damn it was hard.

Eric

Friday, October 29
2:14p.m.

Oh good I'm glad! You're welcome!

Glad to have you back!
Beth

Friday, October 29
3:20p.m.

Hey Beth

there's this halloween fundraiser thing on Sunday that the soccer team is throwing. It won't just be the soccer team, but idk it might be fun. Do you want to go?

No pressure or anything.

Eric

Friday, October 29
3:21p.m.

like with me. If you want.

Eric

Friday, October 29
3:23p.m.

Hey Eric!

I'd love to go :)

Btw my # is 421-859-3386

Beth

LIKE THIS

Valerie Kemp

It is like this.

The boy walks by in that way the cute ones have. You know, half-loping, half-strutting. Head high, eyes all around. Not sure if they're the watcher or the watched, but not really concerned. Either one must be good. Because life is good.

His life, anyway.

And she sits, breath half-held, half-swallowed. Frozen in that state of "casual"—the one that always looks forced. Cursing herself for being so obvious. Cursing him for not noticing.

Why are they all so oblivious? She wonders, absently striking a pose of disheartened fury. If there is such a thing. She probably just invented it now—her awkwardness always creating something unheard of. She is beautiful that way, but doesn't know it. A blessing and a curse . . . or maybe just the way it has to be.

He smiles, crooked teeth and all. So imperfect he cannot be improved upon. It's unfair, she thinks, that two odds make an even, and two evens make an even, but the odd that is her is made up of incomplete parts. She is all halves and quarters—unfinished despite so many pieces. Too many to figure out what's missing.

No, she thinks and boldly points at him inside her mind. *He's* missing.

As if he felt her imaginary finger, he turns. Eyes that seem to know so much more about the world than she ever will catch on hers for the briefest of moments, but a *moment*, still.

An old love song she learned in Spanish class, "Contigo en la Distancia," floats through her mind and she thinks (always thinking) *yes*. That's it. Someday, somewhere, they will come together. The imperfect perfect and the just imperfect. He will fill her empty spaces. Put her together like the jigsaw puzzle she believes she is.

Yes, she thinks again, and remembers to breathe. The gasp rises from her sharply, pushing its way to the ceiling. The place where dreams sit waiting. Where, if you can reach, you can pluck them down and turn them into a tangible thing.

She watches the flawed boy continue on his way. The blandest of scenery in the journey that is his life. He tilts his head back, staring into the dreamspace with a faraway look, and all at once she understands. She knows what she must do to make her dream reality.

For the first time in an eternity, she smiles even though no one is watching. It's simple (she thinks, and feels her heart flutter).

She must learn to fly.

PETALS FALLING

Rieko Mendez

THE MONOCHROME DOORS TO THE express train seal shut inches from me. My hand helplessly reaches out as passengers, pressed close to the window, peer out impassive like a black and white photo. The second bell blares for the train to depart, a signal to step away from the platform's edge. But I stand there, breathing hard from the run down the worn stairs, willing the doors to open.

I grip my hands. The next train from Tama Station to Tokyo won't be for thirty minutes. At this rate, I'm going to miss my mom's walk. I blink; the image of her frail face, smiling and saying it's okay, sits heavy in my chest. My broken promise hangs limp by my side while the train's gray doors become one streak of silver, a rumbling accelerating, kicking up wind and scent of rusty rails and old dirt.

A hand grabs my arm and pulls me back as the end of the train roars past and into the tunnel, the square diminishing like an infinity mirror print. I was so sure I'd make it on the express—my mind had already left on the train while leaving the rest of me behind.

The draft from the train buffets against me. The ringing from the train's thunder dissipates as the platform's edges take shape.

"Are you all right?" The hand releases my arm.

My heart flips.

"Jamie?"

Warmth flushes up my face at saying his name, thoughts of the train and home flying out. The Jamie on the cross-country team. The Jamie with the sideways smile. The Jamie that doesn't know me or how I feel about him.

"Looks like we both missed the express. ASIJ?"

My jeans and backpack make it obvious I go to the American School In Japan. Also, there's something un-Japanese about how I move—that's what my Japanese cousins say. I haven't figured out if that's a compliment or just different.

I nod, never this close to those amber eyes. My fingers at my side trace how his eyes curve with an urge to sketch his face. I prefer the traditional black for charcoal, but I have an impulse to try a sanguine reddish brown. So many cross-country meets to say hello, but he's always surrounded by friends. The closest I got was handing him an icepack. The team dropped to second place the next meet when he couldn't run. He's that good—not just at running but also rallying the team. I would have stayed running to see him if it weren't for my love of art—argh—the culprit, why I'm late.

I refocus and grip my backpack straps. "Thanks." With the weight of missing the express sinking in, I need to move before my feet get mired to the ground. I begin drifting down the length of the platform.

All those hours of painting and nothing to show for. I rub my temples, hoping to clear the web of shadows that's been obscuring my colors—the colors that normally flit and swirl and deepen like music.

Breathe, breathe.

"Hey, wait up." Jamie's footsteps catch up from behind.

My brain scrambles. I stowed away thoughts of Jamie with my cross-country uniform last year. Art. School. Home. That's all the space I have in my chest. He's not supposed to be talking to me. He's never spoken to me. He's Jamie, the star cross-country runner. Now he's chasing me down the platform.

I swallow and stop walking.

A recognition lights his face. "Hey, I remember you. From one of the meets last year. You're the one that got me that icepack."

My eyes widen that he remembers, considering all of us varsity girls look alike in our ponytails and black and gold uniforms. Jamie is talking to me, and he remembers me. The feelings I had so carefully wrapped and shelved begin to unravel.

As his brows gather in the silence, I fumble for words.

Then I catch myself.

Get a hold of yourself. Remember you stopped being a silly girl with crushes. It's senior year. You've got more important plans.

I square my shoulders. "Hi, I'm Mei."

He throws his sideways smile. "Hi, Mei. Training late too?"

My heart dips a notch. "Oh." Of course, he hasn't noticed I no longer run with the team. *Focus on your plans.* "No. I'm not doing cross-country this year."

He tilts his head.

"I was working on my art."

The evening's indigo descends in layers over the deep golden pink of the day. My fingers twitch—the need to capture every shade, wave, light. Colors. My ally. My escape. Sunset with a silhouette of a receding train would add to my Tokyo portfolio. But first, I've got to finish my sunrise series.

Breathe. Tomorrow.

"Like, as in painting?" With his hand behind his neck, he seems less sure what to say. I've never seen him out of sorts.

"I'm working on a portfolio for the annual Tokyo Art Exhibit." My heart quickens at my own words. Besides the art teacher, I haven't told anyone about it.

"Sounds serious." He straightens his gaze at me. Like he's seeing me in a different light.

I bite my lower lip, unsure why I decided to tell him. It's like we're the only ones caught in this pocket of time between day and night. The platform stands mostly empty except for a mom with a toddler at the far end.

"Every other year, junior artists get to submit entries for an opportunity to be in the exhibit." I take a deep breath. "This would be my last chance before graduating high school."

"You must be really good."

My cheeks warm at his compliment. "We'll see."

"I'm sure you work hard at being great at art. I can hear it in your voice." He gazes out to the low hanging sun—the golden hour when anything seems possible.

Gold shimmers in the air.

His words hit a chord inside me. "Sounds like you know what that's like," I say.

He takes a deep breath, his shoulders rolling into place. "I'm like that when it comes to running so I get it." He turns to me and his face lights up. "Maybe I'll see you on the late train again."

The last of the sun warms my face. "Maybe."

The magic of the golden hour with Jamie flutters into the night like fairy dust embers. Hidden in my chest, the candle flame of a dream flickers bright. *I want to be an artist*—there. I said it—rather I thought it. Jamie seemed to get it—how a seed of a dream begins to grow inside us, wanting out. I want to be me. I want to take flight.

It's already nighttime dark when I get off the train. The windows of our apartment stare back black when I walk up to our building.

My chest tightens. All the sun, stars, and light flicker out of me, leaving a thick blackness pooling heavy in my chest. An image of my mom's kind smile—it's always a kind smile—pops in my mind. She knows how busy I am. She's got to be getting better.

But my feet hasten. I'm already sweating under my jacket from half-running, half-walking home from the station, my back sore from carrying my text books.

"Mom, I'm home." I kick off my shoes at the entry and slide off my backpack with a thud. I switch each light on as I hurry to her room.

"Mei, oka-eri, good to have you home." Mom is propped against a pillow on her bed, her prayer book in her hand.

"Sorry—"

"No sorry necessary." There's that kind smile. "Come sit here for a minute."

As I lower on the bed, my heart begins to slow down. I hadn't realized it was beating so hard. Her face isn't as pale as it has been the last few months and I even catch light dancing in her eyes. She's getting better—of course, she's getting better.

I give her a smile.

Her hands, thin and soft, cup my hand. "How's the painting?"

My breath hitches. "How did you know—" As soon as I ask, I notice the bits of paint stains on my hand where my washing missed. "Good.

I…I have some projects to finish for class." My dream flickers in my chest, still too frail to open its windows.

Mom holds my gaze. "Painting has always been in your heart."

WITH THE SCENT OF THE sweet broth, I take a break from homework and stroll to the kitchen.

The warm light from the door and the sounds of water and clatter, familiar, ease my chest after weeks of the dark and quiet kitchen. Mom is getting better. I release a long sigh, the tightness harbored in my hand finally relaxing. *Indigo. More indigo.* That's what I need for the painting. For the first time in weeks, the colors break through in my mind like reaching the summit of a mountain. My hand flutters as if brushing the canvas.

Mom stands in the narrow aisle of our small kitchen, rinsing spinach. Her dress hangs loose, her frame thinner than the last time I remember. It's been a long time since I cooked with her.

"Do you need any help?" I'm surprised my voice shakes.

A smile fills her face and all those times I stood with her in the kitchen—taking in how to slice an onion without tears, how to rub the ends of a sliced cucumber—well up inside me.

"You can help get the electric pot on the table. It's sukiyaki. Less chopping and cooking for me." She winks.

With the jingle of keys and rustle at the door, Dad is home.

We sit with the warm steam of the sukiyaki bubbling at the center of the table. We're finally back to a dinner of three.

"How was the walk?" Dad says.

My stomach tightens, the image of the express train disappearing into the tunnel.

"No walk today—it's too cool anyway." My mom smiles, but her hand trembles as she adds more beef slices to the pot.

Before I catch myself, I make my stupid promise again. "We can walk next week. There's still time, right?"

"'Petals falling, Unable to resist, the moonlight.' Yosa Buson cherry blossom haiku." My dad, visiting Japanese literature professor, reflects on his love of Japan. His eyes soften towards Mom. "Maybe." Then he turns to me. "As long as there's no rain or wind."

I grip my hands, the haiku suddenly taunting me for being late. But the painting—it's important.

The bold of indigo shifts restless inside me.

"Cherry blossoms are so fragile," I say. "They…they don't last. But, daisies bloom all summer. And dandelion can survive anywhere."

I miss the open green fields of upstate New York where we used to live. People in New York say what they mean. No second-guessing any message behind the words. Maybe I'm just too American.

My mom reaches for my hand and I stiffen, but she keeps holding it. There's a sturdiness in her frail gentleness, a sureness I've always known as a little girl.

"They're not as fragile as you think." The warmth is back in her cheeks.

Her calm washes over me.

My dad covers his hands over ours. "The essence of sakura, cherry blossom. Samurai favored the sakura for its fierce ephemeral existence." Hope rises in his voice.

THE FOLLOWING WEEK, WITH MORE color in Mom's cheeks and her moving in the kitchen, I double down on my Tokyo portfolio.

I switch to the larger 24" x 36" canvas to showcase the skyscrapers. The shades of indigo like the magic of night perfectly silhouette the Tokyo cityscape, against the crimson-tinged sunrise for the country of the rising sun. Mom will like my choice of the sunrise. I imagine her smile. I vow to take her to the exhibit if I qualify. I work late to complete one of the three sunrise panels. Six more weeks until submission deadline.

As I sketch, waiting for the late train, someone slides next to me on the bench. I catch a scent of grass and citrus and my pulse quickens.

"Jamie." I figured he had caught the express train when I hadn't seen him on the platform.

"Looks like we've both been working hard." He sits awfully close.

A tingle runs up my whole body. But I refocus on my sketch. "How was practice?"

He stretches his legs out and leans his head back. "Good. I don't think I can go one day without running."

His face catches the golden sun, a serene smile towards the sky. It's the kind of smile that takes over me when I'm painting—really painting.

"What does running feel like to you?" I sit sideways to face him.

He sits up and his amber gaze fixes on me. "It's like…like I become the wind, the cloud, the sky…like I'm flying. It's like I'm free to be me."

His words fill my chest—exactly how painting makes me feel—like I'm free to be me.

I work late the next three days to complete the second of the sunrise panels. Jamie shares his plans to go to college in California, his dream of making the Olympics track and field team. I share my dream of going to art school and becoming an artist.

On the fifth night that week, I find Dad's shoes and that of a stranger at the entry. It's early for Dad to be home. My chest tightens and I hasten down the hall.

My dad walks out of the bedroom with Dr. Matsumoto. "Mei."

"Is she okay?"

He gives a quick glance towards the doctor, whose brows furrow as he dips his head to me. "She's resting. I'll be back after I see the doctor out."

I hurry to the bedroom—the bedside lamp, the only light in the room, and the dark seeping in through the windows like an unwanted guest.

"Mom." My voice is a whisper. I sit on the edge of the bed.

She smiles, but her face is pale, no longer the warm glow from yesterday. "Mei, oka-eri."

My throat constricts. She's supposed to be getting better.

"What happened?"

She slides herself up against the pillow. "A little tired." Her hand covers my paint-stained one. "I did a little walking and got tired."

My breath gets caught in my chest. My promise to take her on her walk sinks heavy inside me. She was getting better. I've been caught up in the exhibit deadline. If only the cherry blossoms bloomed longer.

"What is it about the cherry blossoms—" I catch my trembling voice from saying more. Something deep inside me begins to crack.

Her hand remains steady on mine. "The sakura reminds us of the beauty of life. And the courage." She gazes at me, a little glow back in her cheeks. "You're so grown up, Mei.

An urge to stop time from slipping away takes over me. "Mom…I'm going to submit my work to the Tokyo Art Exhibit."

Her smile deepens. "That's wonderful." Light flickers in her eyes. "You've always had a talent for art."

I hang onto her secure grip. "I don't know…my work might not qualify—"

"Life's too short not to try."

The crack inside shifts ever so slightly.

The need to know what she was like at seventeen, how she knew who she wanted to be, what it was like growing up in Japan, how she met Dad—they all flood through me. But my throat tightens.

"Mom, I'm afraid."

The lines beside her eyes crease with the many years of offering a smile to me.

"We're all a bit afraid." She tightens her hand over mine. "But you're more ready than you think."

The indigo stirs inside me and I hold her gaze as long as I can.

There's still time, I decide. Tomorrow. Cherry blossoms.

I TAKE AN EARLY EXPRESS train right after class with plans to stop by cherry blossom lane.

As I exit the station, a dusky gray blankets the city even though it should still be daylight. My stomach tightens. More of the same gray darkens the sky. A breeze stirs and clouds like a thick smoke roll in the horizon.

Petals falling.

My adrenaline kicks in, and I press past the exiting passengers. I hear my phone buzz, but I ignore it. I break through the crowd and start running. It's not too far—I'll make it.

The wind whirls at my feet and lashes up, my hair whipping against my face. I cinch my backpack straps so I can run straighter without the pack bouncing against my back. Office workers tuck their jackets tight, glancing up at the darkening sky while quickening their steps. A flurry of white sweeps down from the sky. My eyes widen. How can it snow in April? But as I extend my hand while running, the soft flakes fly between my fingers. They're not melting.

Cherry blossom petals.

I grip my backpack straps and pick up my pace. As I skid to the left, I turn the corner.

I halt. My breath hitches.

Against the charcoal gray landscape, the rows of cherry blossoms emerge, majestic and unflinching, towering like myriads of brightly lit lanterns aglow in every shade of white and pink. It's like I've stumbled upon the entrance to the land of the faeries, the long lane stretching forward. Their petals tinted with blush fill the air like confetti, reveling in the spring breeze.

They're not so fragile—mom's words echo. They're not afraid.

A moisture dots my face. More dots fall on the gray cement. My pulse quickens.

Rain.

I hasten to the bench below the closest tree. As I reach one of the thinner branches, I clip a piece with its pink blooms.

The putter of raindrops starts low, then louder.

I tuck the branch under the flap of my jacket and dash down the street.

The rain pelts my face. The earthy scent fills my nose. More petals swirl high and far like they're surfing their last wave. Their white pink disperses through the sky, softening the grayness. They accompany me as if to guide me safely home.

I throw my damp shoes and backpack off once inside and stumble down the hall.

"Mom."

Dad at her bedside, turns to me. I tighten my grip over the branch, my heavy breath filling the quiet.

"She's resting." Dad's eyes are wet.

The crack inside me widens, but I return a smile and a nod.

As I kneel by the bed, water drips from my hair onto her comforter.

She whispers, "Mei."

"Mom, cherry blossom." My voice cracks as I extend the thin branch, damp from the rain. A cluster of three blooms remains.

Her eyes flutter but fail to open. Instead, her hand shifts over mine holding the cherry blossom. A glow washes over her face like she's the wind, the cloud.

It rains for three days, the city with new green splashed in unexpected street corners. My hand barely stirs to capture the color of spring that should remind me of renewal. The numbness paves over the crack inside and smudges like white paint added to black that keeps turning gray. I haven't stepped into the art studio since that first day of rain.

The funeral arrives too soon, the rain now a shimmering gray, washing away any color. Black clouds, suits, dresses, and umbrellas descend. The priest's black robe shifts, revealing the black frame housing the photo of my mom's face.

I can't breathe. As soon as it ends, I escape to find my space.

In a blur of a train ride, I find myself before the art room door. I shouldn't be here—I should be home—the thought catches in my throat. She's gone.

The smell of turpentine and paint, familiar, draws me into its refuge. The studio is quiet, the students having left for the day. I enter the room, my feet tentative on the paint-speckled floor, where my dream started. In the corner sits my canvases, untouched since I last left them. I uncover the two sunrise panels and the third blank canvas, placing each on an easel. I mix the paint, but no colors fill my chest. The indigo I loved now stares back flat and inept. All those hours I didn't spend with my mom gape back at me.

My grip around the brush tightens. Only black oozes from the crack inside me. I dip the brush in the paint and begin painting the blank canvas.

She was supposed to get better.

The crack gives way, unable to contain the black that stains my heart. Then the black bubbles and hisses. *Why didn't you get better? Why didn't you try harder?* Heat gathers behind my eyes. With all my strength, I move to the first and second panels, repainting until they're complete.

All three panels, a solid black, mirror the black that fills my chest. I snuff out the selfish flame. I fall to my knees, the brush tumbling from my hand. *I'm sorry.* The tears rain down, my chest heaving. The dread that I'd been carrying for the last months releases in torrents.

School fills each day of the following week to keep the silence at bay, but the black stirs whenever I pass the unlit, quiet kitchen. I resort to picking up takeout bentos for dinner and feign going to bed early to avoid Dad.

When I return home on Friday, I find Dad's shoes in the entry. I stiffen, not wanting to disturb the numbness inside me. With the sound of pots from the kitchen, I escape to my room.

While catching my breath, I spot two slim books on my desk. My throat tightens as I trace the worn cover with Japanese lettering.

My mom's prayer book.

An accordion fold book, the Japanese Buddhist prayer streams up and down the pages. It was with her every day. The second is her book of haiku with its textured washi Japanese paper. My dad's note rests beside them.

I thought you might want to have these. Love, Dad.

The crack I had so carefully stitched closed begins to split. I close my eyes, my mom's kind smile emerging, and press both books against my chest to will the heat and colors back into the crack. I wait for the numbness to return.

"Mei."

My eyes fly open.

Dad stands in the doorway under the hallway light, more wrinkles visible on his normally youthful face.

I shake my head side to side, afraid what sound might come out if I opened my mouth. He walks towards me to give me a hug, but I swallow what rises from the crack and bolt past him and out of the apartment.

I run and run, the two thin books clutched against my chest.

Pedestrians crowding the streets pass in a blur of flesh tones, a mix of yellow ochre, cadmium red, titanium white. Streaks of buildings—color of raw umber, alizarin crimson, and burnt sienna—close in on my side. Cerulean blue peeks in the distance and I sprint.

I skid right and turn the corner.

My breath heaves. Against the blue, the rows of ancient trees stretch their branches, in the place of the pink blooms, rustle leaves—green, a mix of cadmium yellow and cobalt teal.

I collapse onto the bench.

The numbness like a gray marine layer dissolves and every color inside me explodes.

I miss you.

The tears tumble. But this time, they taste like the cyan ocean and shimmer shades of all the colors on the palette. The colors of her smiles.

As I raise my hand to wipe my face, her prayer book tumbles to the ground.

My stomach tightens as the book hits the cement and its accordion pages unfold into the breeze. I dive down to rescue it. As I gather the two ends of the book to refold the panels, lines emerge on the paper. I sit down, dabbing my eyes, and examine it closely. On the blank back side, a detailed pencil sketch fills every panel.

I catch my breath. My fingers tremble, finding a hidden treasure tucked inside. Page by page, I unfold each panel, my eyes widening with each one. The back of the prayer book opens into one big sketch of the cherry blossom trees in full bloom.

My fingers trace the detailed notched five petals of each sakura. Pink flutters on the pages as if shifting in the breeze. The dots of pollen at each center hint at the deep yellow of the sun. How many days had she walked here to sketch her sakura even when she was ill? *Life's too short not to try. You're more ready than you think.*

I rise with her books held against my chest. I couldn't stop her from becoming ill—I now understand that. But I can live each breath I have just like she did. I know who I am now. My chest expands, breathing in the hint of amaretto and green sap of the sakura leaves.

~ ~ ~

I HAVE THREE WEEKS UNTIL the exhibit deadline.

With the help of my art teacher, I gather what I need and work late every day after school.

End of the week, Friday, I sit at the station, eyes closed with the golden sun on my face. Two more weeks until submission deadline—I won't give up.

With the scent of grass and citrus, my eyes fly open.

"Jamie."

He sits beside me. "It's good to see you."

I return a nod and all my feelings reflect deep in his eyes. He knows what it means to work hard at being great at something. He knows I still carry that crack inside me. As I rub the paint clinging on my hands, he covers them with his, sitting beside me.

~ ~ ~

May 30th, my dad takes the day off to help transport my portfolio for submission. I arrange my folder with my artist statement and the written proposal, describing its story. *You are an artist.* My art teacher's unexpected words had filled my chest.

While my dad waits in the car with the artwork loaded, I linger in the safety of the art room. With this day finally here, my heart wavers—my work too bold, too unconventional, not Japanese enough. I rub at the paint on my hands.

Colors flutter in my chest—life's too short to not try. I close my eyes to quell the heat that rises at the back of them. I take in the familiar scent of creation that's guided me this far. Life is about showing up regardless of the outcome.

I close the door of the art room and join my dad.

I fill the next weeks of waiting with finals and more painting, the colors inside me now unstoppable.

~ ~ ~

The call comes earlier than expected. *We welcome you to join this year's Tokyo Art Exhibit.*

I step into the Tokyo Art Exhibit.

My heart quickens as I approach the junior artists' hall.

I catch my breath. My large sakura panels grace one whole wall. The washi paper flutters fragile and yet flows valiant across the indigo panels like wind, like river. Their yellow dots of pollen, fireflies in space, glow like the start of dreams in our hearts.

A ribbon is pinned by my name. *Capturing the Japanese Spirit Award.*

I rub the paint on my hands. Just when I step into my own, I discover what it means to be Japanese. *Samurai favored the sakura for its fierce ephemeral existence.*

"Congratulations." Jamie's arm brushes against mine, scent of grass and citrus in the air.

My cheeks warm. "You came."

His hair is combed down and he stands taller in his button-down shirt and slacks. But light dances in the same amber eyes. "I knew right away these are yours."

A tingle runs up my arm for what of me he sees in my art. "How?"

"The indigo," he says. "It makes the whole thing feel bold and flying—like they're…waves. Surfing with the blossoms."

I stare into his face, how much he gets me, how much he knows where I've been and who I've become. Colors fill my chest.

"There's more," I say.

He tilts his head and follows me to the other side of the wall.

Japanese lanterns glow over the smaller panels titled *Friendship.* Silhouettes of two people stand at Tama Station, a sunrise in the background.

Jamie's eyes widen. "That's us."

The silly tears well up. "Arigato, Jamie."

His jaw twitches into a smile. He shifts closer to hold my hand.

I grip his tight. We face the panels, every emotion from those times swirling inside me. I had found the heart of Japan—the subtle unsaid sorrows, kindnesses, and beauty of what life means.

As I step out of the building, the lingering spring breeze brushes against my cheeks. White sweeps from the sky.

My heartrate picks up. It's past the season—yet a flurry of sakura petals swirl through the air, the faint scent of amaretto and green wrapping around me. All the colors wash over the crack that I now know will always be there.

SAY MY NAME LIKE A PRAYER

CeCe Heard

"but you believe in God"
as if
God
didn't
create
me this
way
as if God and queerness can't exist in the same holy temple
as if God isn't the embodiment of queered existence
God
who
created
man
and
woman
in Their
image
God
whose
image
contains
both
man
and
woman
God a nonbinary supreme
as if God Them self isn't love
as if love isn't love
as if I was deceived
as if I fell in love with
the devil in sheep's clothing
as if I am the devil
in sheep's clothing
as if I am a punishment
for your transgressions
as if I am your own personal hell
as if I am the fire
to baptize your sin
as if I was created
to judas you to salvation
I judas you to hell
I judas you to temporal damnation
I judas I judas
I judas
—say my name like a prayer

THE NIGHT SEARCH

Andrea Lianne Grabowski

YOUR BACKPACK DRAGS DOWN YOUR shoulders as you follow Harlow out of school, the October air filling your chest with indescribable briskness.

Wait for unfamiliar boys to clear out of the bike rack before retrieving your own. Wheel it over to where she stands.

Say, “Well, bye for now, I guess.” You don’t want to leave her.

A smirk creeps onto Harlow’s mouth. “Who says we have to part ways?” She adjusts the strap of her patched-over canvas shoulder bag, each patch embroidered or painted herself.

“I—nobody.” You feel a bit silly. A scrap of chilly wind flings your hair into your eyes.

Harlow reaches out and tucks it behind your ear. She’s taller than you, maybe bordering on five foot eight, but it’s hard to tell with the array of heeled boots she wears. Her dyed-crimson hair is mostly bunched into a snarly bun with a bandana tied around it, but the wind buffets the escaped strands. “I could come back to your house?”

Think of the mess inside, your mom's wine bottles on the counter, the broken screen door.

"Whatever we do, I *don't* want to go home," Harlow continues. "I could at least walk you back?"

So you wheel your bike in the direction of your neighborhood, Harlow walking beside you, bracelets clinking at the edge of her leather jacket sleeves as she dissects her classes.

Harlow is a senior, just turned eighteen. You won't be seventeen for three more months. Sometimes you feel like you're the same age, like everyone in your grade is so goddamn *naive.* But sometimes you feel like a child, like when Harlow talks about everyone she slept with or dated before her current boyfriend, Brandon. You've only ever dated your boyfriend Trent, a straight-As nerd with sandy hair and the softest eyes. Brandon is—the opposite of Trent. Dark-haired and tattooed, drifting at the edges of school grounds, your twin brother's weed dealer.

Pause, rest your bike against your hip, zip up your own leather jacket. Harlow stops with you, dark-rimmed eyes squinting as she smiles.

You haven't been hanging out for long. You've known who she is, of course—heard the fucked-up things people whispered about her in the halls, saw flashes of her turquoise hair, noticed when she and Brandon became inseparable last year.

But the first week of junior year, Harlow burst in late to the math class you were dreading, new hair the color of poppies, and the only empty seat was beside you.

"You're Harper's sister, right?" she'd whispered.

Of course Brandon would be the kind of guy to call his friends by their last name. Harlow was leaning so close, it was overpowering. But not in the invading-personal-space overpowering you usually feel. No, this was something else. You nodded.

"Nice shirt," Harlow had said. "Dani."

So she knew your name, not just who you were related to. And she liked Black Veil Brides. And then the math teacher put you together for group work, and there was no going back.

It quickly became much less about algebra and much more about music, clothes, anything else. It feels easier to laugh than it has in months. It feels like your social circle is expanding. It feels like you're less afraid of people.

Just last week you and your brother, Nat, ran breathlessly after Harlow and Brandon through the grocery store in your neighborhood, grabbing snacks and carrying them to the closest park, the one with the lead-infested swing set. It was almost midnight, and the four of you lay sprawled on the grass, cigarettes glowing like fireflies. Well, you didn't have your own, they make you cough too much, but sometimes you took drags from Harlow's. It was oddly compelling to place your mouth where hers had been. It made you feel as if you were exchanging some sort of secret communication outside of the boys' banter.

Beside you, she's run through her complaints. She laughs hoarsely and nudges your arm. "But what about your day, Dani?"

You shake your head. "Nat being given detention was the only exciting thing."

Harlow sighs. "Brandon too. Fuck this place." She raises a middle finger behind her as if you've not left the school in your wake already.

Turn onto your street. You're used to going to Trent's after school, but today he has a meeting with an adviser about dual enrolling at the community college in the winter. He wants to become an astronomer, is already looking at universities.

You have no idea what you want to do.

"Well, here we are." Roll your bike into the cracked driveway, fish out your keys. Your hands tremble a little with anxiety as you unlock the door and the two of you walk into the small living room and kitchen area.

She puts her hands on her hips appraisingly. "And we have this place to ourselves for how long?"

Your face is hot. "Mom should be getting home a little after four." Set your backpack on the threadbare couch and peek in some cupboards. "Do you—do you want popcorn?"

She is startlingly close behind you. "Hell yeah."

Your mom does not get home from work around four. Not even at five. You sit eating popcorn and there is barely any space between her thighs and yours.

Harlow gets a text from Brandon—he's busy, and with Nat.

"Works out well for us, then." Harlow kicks her feet up on the edge of the scuffed coffee table. She hasn't said a word about the house. But of course she wouldn't. She's your first girl friend since before middle school who's equally poor.

She's not Blake, that's for sure. Not going to be surprised about anything.

Smile, eat the last puffed grain in your bowl, set it on the floor.

But worry creeps in. Fidget with your locket from Trent. Text your mom: *did you go to Clay's?* Clay is her newest boyfriend. You like him better than the other ones. They have never been *villainous,* but none of them have been as kind to your mom as Clay. And he doesn't try to be a dad to you and Nat.

Try to distract yourself by asking Harlow questions about her latest sewing projects. She's transformed so many thrifted items into the best sort of additions to her punk-femme wardrobe. She shows you pictures, but you eye the clock on her phone. Nearly six. And there's nothing from your mom.

"Your face looks pinched," Harlow says teasingly. "Something bugging you?"

Rub your forehead. Familiar tightness constricts inside you. The ache for relief, the almost *desperation* of it. "Um, just concerned my mom isn't home yet."

"You don't *want* her to be home, though, do you?" Harlow asks.

It's true. You want to sit here alone with Harlow on the couch for hours more. Delay your answer by texting Clay—it's only the second time you've sent him a message, and you feel weird about it.

"Not exactly, but she—she's kind of disappeared a couple times."

Harlow scoots closer, thigh pressed against yours now. "What do you mean?"

Stare at your hands in your lap. Your black nail polish is chipped beyond any aesthetic appeal.

Harlow gets it. You let it slip last week, the fact that your mom's been drinking so much for years. It surprised you, since it took so long to tell Trent back when you were in middle school and simply friends playing video games with Nat. But you knew you could say it to Harlow the moment she started griping about her dad's gambling. Still, your words come haltingly now.

"She—she doesn't have friends, really, that she'd hang out with. And I know I should just believe she's running errands or something, but last year… she stormed out of the house and instead of just pacing around the yard she drove to some random parking lot on the other side of town, got so drunk, just right there in the car, that she fell asleep. Nat and Trent and I spent hours looking for her."

Harlow puts her hand on your knee. "Shit, Dani. Of course you're worried now."

"That wasn't the only time, either." You're so conscious of her hand. "Once, the cops found her first. And Nat has to pick her up at bars sometimes."

Harlow nods. "Done that for my dad a few times, the picking up part. But fuck, never this *mystery*."

Your phone buzzes with a text from Clay. *Haven't talked to or seen her all day, sorry.* Show Harlow the screen.

She lifts her hand and sits up straighter. "Well, should we go look for her?"

"I—well, you don't have to. I should just call Nat."

Harlow returns her hand to your knee. "Oh, let's not get the boys involved. We can go sleuthing. It'll be okay."

Place your hand over hers for just a second. "Okay."

Just to be safe, you text Nat again. *where you at?* He replies instantly. *just chilling in the park.*

A fragment of relief pushes you up off the couch to go back to your room for the warmer of your leather jackets and a scarf. Remember how long you drove around with Nat and Trent last year, and grab a beanie too.

Dig your fingernails into your palms. The desperation rises, stifling your breath. Stare at the poster for your favorite band, Less Than Well. Akihiko Masashi's face is staring back at you, a fierceness in his expression, freedom in the long hair flying mid-rise from headbanging. He has watched you all throughout this year of fogginess, sharp things, control, fitful sleep. His guttural voice *sang* you through it, more like. Because he knows what it is to experience this.

You can just walk out. You can walk right into the evening with Harlow by your side and forget about this feeling. Can't you?

"Dani!" Harlow calls. "Do you have a flashlight?"

Let out a breath. "I'll look!"

Force yourself back to the living room.

Harlow has pulled her hair down and tied her bandana around her head in a triangle, knotted under her hair. "I know, I know, I look like I walked out of *Fiddler on the Roof*," she says, giggling. "But it's warmer."

You can't help laughing too. There's a flashlight under the sink, and it turns on, but you have no idea how long the batteries might last.

"I have pepper spray," she says. "We're armed and ready."

First you check the bars within walking distance. Nothing. Harlow jokes about her fake ID as you walk out of the third and last one on your mental list. You can't laugh. You feel young, small beside her.

"She works down there, right?" Harlow points a street over to one of the busier, four-lane roads that snake through town.

"Well, kind of." You head down a side street to get to that road. "It's in that stretch of warehouses. So like, a few more miles."

"But she wouldn't stay at work, right?"

Shake your head. Your mom just got this job in August, after an excruciating month of applications, pleading with the landlord, you working your ass off at your own job. The only mercy of that space between your mom's firing and being hired was that it was summer. You and Nat free to earn the money she couldn't.

"The night shift comes in right after she's done," you tell Harlow. "She wouldn't be allowed to stay for more hours."

Harlow nods, untying her bandana and running her hands through her hair, then retying it.

"But—" You pause on the sidewalk, the main road just a few steps away. "She's always so tired. Maybe she just fell asleep in her car after work." Start walking again, faster. "The—"

"The bus stop," you and Harlow say at the same time.

It's a welcome warmth to step onto the bus when it arrives. It carries you to the next stop, a few blocks before the businesses start petering out and desolate grass-and-gravel mark the empty lots between industrial buildings.

Your theory is futile. Tracing the parking lot for your mom's rusty Toyota Corolla—the same one you and Nat rode around in as toddlers while she played Bratmobile and Veruca Salt cassettes with the windows open—holds a sense of hope for a few minutes. But then a security guard yells at you and you scramble off the property and into the easement, heart pounding.

It's dark by now, but the streetlights provide enough of an eerie glow to see by. Your feet hurt. Keep going anyways, out of the easement and along the sidewalk.

"So…" Harlow draws the word out. "When she stormed out that one time. Or the other times she like, disappeared. Was she upset about something specific?"

Let out a breath. "No… She's just been very volatile ever since she started drinking more."

"You were what, eleven?" Harlow asks.

You are surprised she remembers. "Yeah. Maybe erratic is a better word. Like she'll start drinking, get all upset about some random thing, yell about it until she can't talk straight, and go to bed. But in the morning she's all nice. Sometimes."

It sounds like a pattern the way you're explaining it. And you know that it is. But it feels more like *no* pattern, living on edge all the time. Like you never know when she'll explode or when she'll disappear into her room with a bottle of gin and leave you and Nat to your own peaceful devices.

Harlow nods. "Shit, babe. That's rough."

The word climbs inside you, a radiant coal. You don't know how to respond. So you just keep walking.

"It's past dinnertime," Harlow says. She pulls a patched leather wallet from her bag and flips it open, gesturing with it to the McDonald's back towards the bus station. A few places down from it is a liquor store. "I'll treat us to burgers? Picnic on the road?"

You *are* kind of hungry. "I have money too, I—"

Harlow shakes her head. "It's fine!" She grabs your hand and pulls you down the sidewalk to the intersection. She doesn't let go as you walk across, and adrenaline creeps into you as she tugs you into the empty drive-through lane.

"What are you doing?"

She gestures at the menu board. "I don't want to go inside and face people."

Something about standing here trembling with cold and enunciating your orders into the little speaker is wildly absurd, and you clap your hand over your mouth to keep from giggling as Harlow gives her order. It must be the anxiety. You check your phone again. Nothing.

The guy at the window is around Harlow's age. His eyes get wide and he bursts out laughing. "Why don't you girls come inside and eat? I'm almost done with my shift."

Harlow scrunches her face up. "No thanks," she says bitterly, grabbing the paper bags from him.

"Aw, come on!" He raises his eyebrows suggestively.

Historically, you have not been this brave. You usually let everyone else do the talking. But you spit it out: "Just fuck off!" Grab Harlow's hand, and run into the night.

When you slow down, your breaths come in short gasps. Harlow beams at you, face illuminated by a flickering streetlight.

"Proud of you," she says, kicking aside stray, dried leaves.

"Ha!" But you think of Jo at Café Delgado, the coffee shop you work at: a gangly enby whose speech is peppered with affectionate Spanish. "My manager just started dating someone who's teaching them tae kwon do. They offered to teach me some moves."

"Damn!" Harlow is excited. "You said yes, right?"

You unwrap your burger. "I said maybe. But—next time I work, I could say yes."

The burger's warmth fills your insides, makes you feel a little less like a husk of something. But then your phone buzzes, and your heart starts racing again. It's just a text from Trent. *how you feeling?* He does this often, did it even before you started dating. But especially this last year. Sometimes it's the blatant question, sometimes just an emoji of a fish, because you're a Pisces, or photos of comets. He humors you with that fish. He might have his head in the stars, but he knows they're just flaming balls of gas.

Trent would be ready to hop in his sister's car and get over here. He always makes you feel better, but the idea of sharing sidewalk space with Trent *and* Harlow? You would feel caught between them in the strangest way, like you did at school that one time Harlow hugged you from behind while you and Trent talked at his locker. They're the two safest people at school, but your anxiety spiked, focus bouncing between Trent's smile and the feel of Harlow's arm slung over your shoulder.

Turn his question around and type: *how are YOU? how was the advising meeting?* Slip your phone back into your pocket before he can reply.

The empty lot by the McDonald's, towards the bus station, is empty for a reason—the old railroad crosses here. Start walking on the track, the rhythm of your careful steps calming you. Harlow's walking in tandem on the other track, until she's not, and she's behind you, and you've both stopped, and she's drawing your arms out wide, weaving her fingers between yours. Now, there's no Trent to distract you, no school-induced tension. There's just this space your bodies create in the darkness, her chin tucked into your beanie, wind rustling the leaves around the old rails.

You want to keep walking, forget your mom didn't come home, as if you don't have this weight of responsibility, as if—

As if Trent and Brandon were not waiting for you both somewhere outside of this moment.

Harlow lets go of one of your hands and slides the flashlight out of your jacket pocket. She clicks it on and it catches the rails in its spill.

"Holy shit—" Harlow lifts the light higher. There's a car parked just out of an alley and into the scruffy grass. A rusted silver 1998 Toyota Corolla with a mismatched mirror, belonging to one Heather Harper.

You rush forward and out of Harlow's touch to peer through the passenger window. Your mom is asleep, driver's seat tilted back, a bottle in the cupholder, a crumpled bag that must have been from the very same McDonald's.

Harlow huffs out a breath behind you. "We did it."

You don't feel relief. Turn back to face Harlow. She's startlingly close. "I don't have my driver's license yet," you say.

"I do. We can wake her up, get her in the back seat. I'll drive."

A surge of resistance. It should be *you* driving this car, because it is always you, or Nat, looking after your mom.

But Harlow is already leaving your side and trying the driver's side door. It's locked. She bangs on it, and after a moment you knock on the passenger side, and finally your mom blearily looks up. She sees you first, her dark hair so like yours around her face, and she looks horrified. She fumbles for the lock and Harlow tugs the door open.

"Dani, Dani, I'm sorry, please," your mom mumbles, rubbing her eyes. "God, what—who—"

This is exactly how she behaved when you found her with Nat and Trent. This *cluelessness.* This begging for forgiveness.

It hits you that this will go on and on forever.

You will have to become very used to it.

"Just get in the back seat, Mom," you say quietly. "Harlow's gonna drive us home."

Your mom will go missing again in a few months. You and Trent will find her and the inevitability will sink deeper into your bones. Harlow will make you a necklace with the logo for your favorite band: a caduceus and a heartbeat. You will get your driver's license. Brandon will begin to tattoo a passionflower across Harlow's shoulder, so she in turn gives one to you: a comet. She'll kiss your cheek, spend a night curled into you on your bed. It won't be the last night like it this winter.

Trent will attend early college, and when the leaves bud pale green and snow melts and drips from the gutters, you'll be less in need of Akihiko to pull you out of your fogs. Nat will spend more and more time with Brandon. But come graduation, the older boy will have a new car, a more closed-off look on his elfin face, and it will no longer be just your mom who does the disappearing, but Harlow too.

CONTRIBUTORS

Maia Cataldo is a Boston-based playwright and fiction writer. After graduating from Brandeis in 2020 with a double major in English and Theater, she set her sights on pursuing an MFA in Creative Writing. In addition to being a part time grad-applicant, Maia is the Box Office Manager at the Lyric Stage Company of Boston and nanny to two vivacious readers. Recently, her play *Precious Stuff* was selected and produced for the 2022 Boston Theater Marathon. She is excited to have her first fiction publication, "Our Correspondence," featured in *Just Above Water*. Find Maia on IG: @maia_cataldo.

Andrea Lianne Grabowski is a Midwestern lesbian writer occupying Anishinaabe land. She is a graduate of Northwestern Michigan College and served on the staff of their literary magazine. Her published work lives in *HELL IS REAL Anthology, fifth wheel press, superfroot mag,* and elsewhere. The characters in "The Night Search" have been by Andrea's side for around a decade of growth, and she plans to publish novels with them in the near future. In the meantime, you can find her making zines, on long drives being inspired by music, or peering in the windows of abandoned buildings. Find Andrea on IG: @andrea.lianne or Twitter: @pingouinwrites.

CeCe Heard (she/her/hers) uses the art of storytelling to explore the world around her while expressing the world of thought within herself. She uses her craft to give voice and power to herself and those who share her experiences and/or identities. CeCe is a resident of Columbus, Ohio and a recent graduate of Washington University in St. Louis. Her work has been published by Queer26 and *Voyage YA*, and she has an upcoming piece in *The Worcester Review*. Find her on Twitter and Instagram: @ceceee863.

Kim Johnson held leadership positions in social justice organizations as a teen and in college, and is now an author and vice provost at the University of Oregon. She maintains engagement in various organizations while also mentoring Black student leaders and serving as a graduate advisor and member of a historically Black sorority. *This Is My America* is her bestselling novel that explores racial injustice against innocent Black men who are criminally sentenced, and the families left behind to pick up the pieces. Her novel, *Invisible Son,* will be available in June 2023. She is an award-winning novelist, with 2021 accolades that include the Pacific Northwest Book Award and Malka Penn Human Rights Award for Children's Literature. She holds degrees from the University of Oregon and the University of Maryland, College Park.

Valerie Kemp writes speculative and contemporary fiction for all ages. Her short stories have been published in *Apex Magazine*,

Cast of Wonders, *Voyage YA*, and the HarperTeen anthology *Defy the Dark*. She is a 2022 graduate of Viable Paradise and a recipient of the 2022 Highlights Foundation Community Connections Scholarship. Valerie is a recovering academic whose research focused on the importance of media representation, something she cares deeply about. Find her @ valeriekwrites on Twitter and IG and at valeriekemp.com.

Having spent a lifetime travelling the globe, **Kate Larkindale** currently resides in Wellington, New Zealand. With a full-time job working on festivals and experiences and being a mother to two sons, she's surprised she finds any time to write, but doesn't sleep much. She is the author of YA contemporary novels *An Unstill Life*, *Stumped*, *The Sidewalk's Regrets,* and *Chasing The Taillights* and her short stories have appeared in *Halfway Down The Stairs*, *A Fly in Amber*, Daily Flash Anthology, *The Barrier Islands Review*, *Everyday Fiction*, *Death Rattle*, *Drastic Measures*, *Cutlass & Musket,* and *Residential Aliens*, among others. Find Kate on Twitter and IG: @vampyr14.

Madelin A. Medina is a Dominican-American poet and writer based in Queens, New York where she resides with her husband and two sons. She received her BA in English from Hofstra University. Her work has appeared in *Newtown Literary, The Acentos Review, [PANK] Magazine, Coffin Bell Journal, What They Leave Behind: A Latinx Anthology* and elsewhere. She is also a recipient of the Nancy P. Schnader Academy of American Poets Award. Find Madelin on IG: @madelin_a_medina.

Rieko Mendez, student at Vermont College of Fine Arts for Writing for Children and Young Adults and a SCBWI member, received special mention for her YA contemporary fantasy at SCBWI-L.A. Writers Day

2021 and publishes blog posts for its regional *Kite Tales* publication. She mentors teen girls in underserved communities on writing while volunteering at WriteGirl, an organization that promotes creativity and self-expression to empower girls. As board chair for Ready, Set, Read, a local literacy nonprofit, she co-authored articles for the 2020 LA Times Reading by 9 Guide. Born in Japan, she finds stories from home make their way into her writing. She is a graduate of Stanford University. Find her on Instagram: @riekomendezwriter or www.riekomendez.com.

Christina Polge is a Raleigh native currently attending UNC-Chapel Hill. When she's not writing, she loves frolicking in meadows, driving really fast through puddles and playing her guitar on the beach. She's so excited to share her work with the world! Find Christina on Instagram: @christina.polge.

Brynne Rebele-Henry's poetry collection, *Autobiography of a Wound*, won the AWP Donald Hall Poetry Prize, was one of *Library Journal*'s Top Fall Poetry Picks for 2018, and was a finalist for the 2019 Publishing Triangle Audre Lorde Award. Her first novel, *Orpheus Girl*, received the 2021 Young Adult Virginia Author Award from the Richmond Public Library and was listed as one of the most anticipated YA novels by Barnes & Noble and Chicago Review of Books. She is the author of a bilingual (English and Slovenian) chapbook, *Vizije Se Začnejo Pri Šestih* (Visions Begin at Six), and a 2021–2022 Fulbright Scholar at the Institute of Anthropological and Spatial Studies, Research Centre of the Slovenian Academy of Sciences and Arts. Her most recent poetry collection, *Prelude,* appeared with the University of Pittsburgh Press and is a finalist for the 2022 LAMBDA Award for Lesbian Poetry.

EDITORS

Racquel Henry is a Trinidadian writer, editor, and writing coach with an MFA from Fairleigh Dickinson University. She spent six years as an English Professor and currently owns the writing studio, Writer's Atelier, in Maitland, FL. In 2010, Racquel co-founded *Black Fox Literary Magazine* where she still serves as an editor, and joined *Voyage YA Journal* as Editor-in-Chief in 2020. Since 2013, Racquel has presented and moderated panels at writing conferences, residencies, and private writing groups across the US. She is the author of *Holiday on Park, Letter to Santa, Christmas in Cardwick, The Write Gym Workbook*, and *The Writer's Atelier Little Book of Writing Affirmations.* Her script, *Christmas Magic at Holly Oaks,* is currently optioned with Rom Com Pictures. Racquel's fiction, poetry, and nonfiction has been published in various literary magazines and anthologies. When she's not writing, editing, or coaching writers, you can find her watching Hallmark Christmas movies.

Marquita Hockaday has a BA in history education, an MED in reading, a PhD in educational leadership, and an MFA in creative writing, which she earned from Fairleigh Dickinson University. After attending FDU, Marquita co-founded *Black Fox Literary Magazine*. She is currently Associate Editor at *Voyage*, a young adult literary journal. Marquita has done freelance developmental editing for fiction and nonfiction manuscripts, and, as an educator, she edits and provides feedback for academic papers. Marquita's short fiction is published in *Oyster River Pages* and *The Start Literary Journal*.

Kip Wilson is the author of young adult verse novels *White Rose* (Versify, 2019), about anti-Nazi political activist Sophie Scholl, *The Most Dazzling Girl in Berlin* (Versify, 2022), set in a queer club in Berlin during the last days of the Weimar Republic, and *One Last Shot* (Versify, 2023), about anti-fascist Spanish Civil War photojournalist Gerda Taro. Kip holds a Ph.D. in German Literature and is an Associate Editor at *Voyage YA*.

Special thanks to the *Voyage* readers:

Jena Brown

Robin Gow

Jeune Ji

Talia Moodley

Jenna Reasner

ABOUT VOYAGE

The Voyage Journal publishes short-form young adult literature. YA is an ever-expanding category of literature that constantly pushes boundaries. While the intended audience of YA is teenagers, almost half of YA readers are adults and *Voyage* is happy to be at the intersection of both groups. We are not interested in publishing a specific genre of YA, but we are interested in quality work by writers from a variety of backgrounds, especially #ownvoices. We are excited about creating a space that supports both emerging and established voices.

Find out more information about *The Voyage Journal* via our website: www.thevoyagejournal.com.

Keep up with *Voyage* on our social media platforms:
Instagram: @voyageya
Facebook: facebook.com/voyageyajournal
Twitter: @voyage_ya
TikTok: @voyageya

www.ingramcontent.com/pod-product-compliance
Lightning Source LLC
Chambersburg PA
CBHW061222210726
48294CB00006B/1941